ABOUT THIS BOOK

Welcome to Havenwood Falls, home to sexy men, strong women, and neighbors who bite. Discover supernatural mystery, thrills, and romance in a place where everyone has a deep, dark, and often deadly secret. This is only but one...

Being the alpha's queen is the last thing Atlas Belham has ever wanted. Yet here she stands, blindfolded and binding herself to a life with a man she's never even met. All for the good of her people.

Harrison Xavier's plans have never included taking a mate, ever. He's perfectly happy to allow his cousin to assume his place as leader, especially as old feuds reignite and the black bear kingdom teeters on the edge of revolution. But when he sees Atlas, his whole world shifts.

Life as a royal and in her new hometown of Havenwood Falls, where nothing is as it seems, test Atlas's resolve, but it's Harrison who tries her the most. It's ultimately up to her to choose—freedom and independence for herself or peace for the kingdom.

ALPHA'S QUEEN

A HAVENWOOD FALLS NOVELLA

LILA FELIX

HAVENWOOD FALLS BOOKS

Forget You Not by Kristie Cook

Old Wounds by Susan Burdorf

Fate, Love & Loyalty by E.J. Fechenda

The Winged & the Wicked by T.V. Hahn & Kristie Cook

Alpha's Queen by Lila Felix

Ink & Fire by R.K. Ryals

Lose You Not by Kristie Cook

Tragic Ink by Heather Hildenbrand

Nowhere to Hide by Belinda Boring

Flames Among the Frost by Amy Hale

Rock Me Gently by Susan Burdorf

From the Embers by Amy Miles

Defying Gravity by Kallie Ross

Break Me Not by Kristie Cook

How the Dead Lie by Stacey Rourke

The Lurkers Within by Danielle Bannister

The Collector: Awakening by Kristie Cook, R.K. Ryals, Belinda Boring & Nadirah Foxx

Addicted to You by Belinda Boring

Affliction Mine by C.J. Pinard

The Ward & the Wanderers by T.V. Hahn

Toil & Trouble by Melissa Wright

Of Salt and Stars by Seven Jane

Redefined by Morgan Wylie

Betrayal Among the Frost by Amy Hale

Forever Loyal by E.J. Fechenda

Fate's Demand by Emily Cyr

The Wu & the Wand by T.V. Hahn

A Demon's Redemption by JD Nelson

Also try the YA line, Havenwood Falls High; the historical paranormal line, Legends of Havenwood Falls; the darker, sexier side of town, Havenwood Falls Sin & Silk; and the local supernatural college, Sun & Moon Academy.

Stay up to date at www.HavenwoodFalls.com

OTHER BOOKS BY LILA FELIX

Emerge

Perchance

The Love and Skate Series

Sparrows For Free

Seeking Havok

Hoax

Doves for Sale

AnguiSH

HeartBreaker

The Forced Autonomy Series

The Bayou Bear Chronicles

His Haunted Heart

Dethroning Crown

Tipping the Scales

The Second Chance Romance Series

Doll of Mine

The Supernatural Chronicles: Skinwalker

To all those who wish to shift and be free like bears.

CHAPTER 1

ATLAS

$\mathcal{T}$he lined white lace blindfold lay across the bed, mocking me. Even the bed mocked me with its pristine white coverings and golden accents along the wrought iron frame.

I wondered if this would be my bedroom—our bedroom.

"Is he that ugly? I don't get this tradition."

My best friend Samantha snickered from the corner of the room. "It would be easier to name the ones we do understand. I think this is more of a Havenwood Falls thing than a shifter thing."

"Is he ugly? Is he mean? Will he hate me? I hope he does." My voice held a desperation I hadn't known I was capable of. At this point, one might expect my mother to speak up and give me a few words of encouragement. As was usual for her, she remained silent, oblivious.

"You do not," Samantha said. "And even if he is ugly, you can just reap the rewards. I mean, there's the status and the money. Hell, if he's that big of a prick, you can get your needs met elsewhere, you know. I'm sure there's a yummy jester around, just waiting to make sure the future alpha's queen is satisfied."

My best friend was not a prude, that was for sure.

"There's no jester, Sam. This isn't the Victorian era."

She scoffed. "Could've fooled me. All these rules . . . and that dress costs more than my rent for the year."

At least she could do that—pay her own rent. I was sure I'd never have to pay another bill while I was here. It was a little thing, but I liked the little things in life.

She was right about the dress. Swarovski crystals and pearls cluttered the lithe fabric from shoulders to hem. The style was modest to the point of almost being old-fashioned. There wasn't an inch of skin from my wrists down to my ankles that peeked out. The lace around my collar was crowned with a string of heavy pearls. They weren't as heavy as the deal I'd made to marry a stranger.

"It isn't worth it."

She turned me around to face her. "Don't say that, Atlas. We both know what this means to our people. The classes won't be divided anymore. There won't be the rich shifters and the poor shifters. You are changing everything. Trust me, it's worth ninety days of pain and punishment." She laughed, but I did not.

I sighed and looked at myself in the mirror. I was a cinnamon bear shifter, and we were considered the lesser of the two types of black bear shifters, even though we were technically the same species. Cinnamon bears simply didn't change from brown to black after puberty. Other than our hair color, we were the exact same bear. My light brown hair glistened in the sun that peeked through the moving curtains. The hairdressers had worked a full three hours on it. They didn't touch the color. It proved what I was and the reason why I was marrying the Black Bear Clan's next alpha.

"I don't want to change everything, Sammy. I just want to find a worthy male who loves me. I don't want to be an example or a bridge. Someone called me that the other day, by the way. She told me 'thank you for being the bridge,' like I was some inanimate thing that people walked over from one side of a dirty river to the other."

I looked at the reflection of my mother, who was already three sheets to the wind and working on the fourth. She didn't care. All she knew was the Xaviers had paid off our mortgage and my student loans —a dowry of sorts. The velvet lounge chair she rested in hugged her hips and gave her an excuse to keep chugging down the rum in her glass.

Sammy's hands were on my shoulders before the crying could start. She always knew when I was about to crack open.

"You're not an inanimate object, and anyway, I heard that Harrison is hot as fuck. And just as a bonus, he has a fine booty, too. They blindfold you so you don't slobber on him during the ceremony."

No matter how hard I tried, there was no fighting Sammy's wit. Plus, the laugh made me feel better—a little. Laughing made my breath captive in the veil that began as an adorned piece atop my head and extended below my chin. I looked like I had a fishing net stretched over my face.

Hot or not, I just wanted to be a nurse, find a mate, buy a house, and have some cubs. "This isn't right. I can't talk to people. I can't make decisions that will affect all of us. What if I fuck everything up?"

"You probably will. But, we all do, right?"

"Yeah, especially you."

"Hey! I kind of like not being perfect."

"I like you not perfect, too." I wrapped my arms around my best friend and hoped to the Creator that it wasn't the last time we would embrace like this. She'd be allowed to visit me, but only when I requested her presence.

Ninety days was all I had to last. That was the stipulation in the agreement. *I didn't know what was going to happen to the kingdom in those ninety days, and frankly, I didn't care.* Their offer of monetary gain and peace among our people was too tempting to pass up—even if I hated every second of this setup.

"It's not that long. I can make it, right?"

She hugged me tighter. She was crying now, too. Her body shook against me as she sobbed. "They let me meet him last night, At."

I pulled back, shocked by her confession. "What the hell? Why didn't you tell me? I was wondering how you knew what he looked like. I thought you were just trying to make me feel better."

"They told me not to. But I couldn't keep it from you. He's . . . he's not what you think. That's all I'm going to say. You won't have any trouble lasting the ninety days. Treat this like a real mating. Trust me."

I did.

I just didn't trust my mate-to-be.

A knock sounded at the door. A pith of a girl in a pale pink dress told us that it was almost time. Almost time to go.

"Well, let's not drag this out." Sammy reached to straighten my veil again and kissed me on the cheeks.

"One day maybe . . ."

"Don't even say it, Atlas. It's just a few days, and then you will be free of this place."

I fisted the sleeve of her dress, not willing to let her go yet.

"All of this is ridiculous. This castle. This wedding. This dress. These rules. What kind of alpha won't let my best friend attend my wedding?"

"It's all about numbers, Atlas. You know that. Your mom will be there along with some servants. That many cinnamon bears under one roof is probably making the alpha squirm enough without adding one more to the mix."

She stepped away, but before her hand touched the door, she looked over her shoulder at me. "You have to change things, Atlas. At the very least, you have to try."

The girl who had summoned me still stood at the door, staring at me as though I'd just given birth to an alien. "Is something wrong?" I asked, checking myself over in the mirror.

"No, ma'am. Is it true? You've come to help us?" Her question was barely audible.

Sammy and I looked at each other in shock. My stomach rolled as I realized the shake in this girl's voice wasn't from speaking to me, but rather what she alluded to.

"I'm going to try."

Trying was the only thing I could promise.

CHAPTER 2

HARRISON

*E*very time my father, the alpha, paced from one side of the room to another, he took a glance at himself in the mirror. It was like watching the most conceited ballerina on the planet.

"Dad, could you please stop? You're making me nervous and frankly driving me bat— Just crazy."

He tossed a look over his shoulder telling me not only would he not stop, but that I'd better shut up about it as well. I learned that look at an early age.

"We have to make this work, Harrison. The people—the lesser ones—they are making it hard on us. They reject our decisions. They resist. We have to earn their trust again, or our dynasty is in jeopardy. I'm not sure you're taking this seriously enough."

What my father didn't understand was that I didn't give a fuck if the dynasty fell down around us and burned to the ground. The only thing I had my sights set on was waiting out the end of my father's reign. Whether it be by death or the frailty of old age, he would have to give up on his tyranny one day, and even if he did offer me the position of alpha, which he would not, I would not accept. I was content to allow Dolrich to take my place as his shadow, hoping that my father would favor him in place of me. Dolrich would be our new alpha, even if my father didn't quite grasp it yet.

Not that he really favored me all that much in the first place.

A knock at the door finally stopped my father from pacing and made me immediately stand at attention. This was it. It was time for me to be married to someone I didn't know.

Ridiculous. All of it.

"It's just me. Stand down." Dolrich opened the door and closed it behind him quickly. He was wearing a similar tux to mine, except my tie and handkerchief were gold, signifying my rank as in line for alpha. His was purple, which showed he was royalty.

I knew that my new mate would be wearing a gold garter underneath her pristine white dress.

Hey, I had to get happy about something in this disastrous day.

"Dolrich, you scared the f— You scared me."

The alpha didn't appreciate vulgar language in his presence. Too bad fuck was my favorite word. The last time I said damn in front of him, he reached over and covered my mother's ears. She didn't even blink an eye. Mother's favorite word was ass.

Dolrich bared his neck a little for the intrusion. "Sorry. I came to wish you luck. I've heard she's a looker. They are almost ready for you."

A looker. Sometimes looks were just not enough.

My dad bowed up. It seemed he took offense at everything anyone said lately, and my cousin wasn't immune to his defensiveness. "You think I would choose anything less for the next alpha? His queen must be honorable and beautiful."

One of Dolrich's eyebrows raised at me. Dad was insane. Plus, I gave zero fucks about being the next alpha. Any other eligible male could have it. Hell, any of them could have this female I was supposed to be joined to in the next hour. It would be a stiff and cold coupling, just like anyone else's in this family.

Royals didn't marry for love. They married for position, or in my case, for political leverage. My father's attitude and general orders that oppressed the lesser bears of our species had been earning him some backlash in the last decade or so. He thought marrying me off to one of them would be a balm to their wounds.

He might have been right.

He might have been off his fucking rocker.

"Of course not, Alpha. I was simply trying to ease my cousin's nerves a little. He's practically shaking," Dolrich replied.

Was not.

My dad crossed his arms over his chest. "There's nothing for him to be nervous about. Alphas don't get nervous. We stand up and get things done. This isn't emotional. It's his duty."

Another knock came at the door. This time all three of us squared our shoulders for the event to come. I knew it was one of the servants before he even spoke.

"It's time, Alpha."

My father nodded once. Thad, my father's private butler, shut the door with a bow.

"Dolrich, do you mind if I have a word with my son before the ceremony? It will be quick. Please tell everyone that we will be there shortly."

Dolrich bowed a little. "Of course, Alpha. Good luck, Harrison."

The bastard winked at me.

I rolled my eyes at him.

As soon as the door was shut, the alpha was in front of me in the body that used to be my father. He was stiff again. His voice grew cold. His eyes emptied. His jaw clenched.

"This is the day you begin your role as the future alpha. Taking this female is your promise to keep those other bears in line. It is a sacrifice, I know, but it has to be done. We can't have an uprising on our hands. There will be time to mate with her, but the blood rites must be done tonight. You understand? I won't be embarrassed by an unmarked daughter-in-law. Is that clear? I mean it this time, Harrison. I realize you don't have the strength or the gumption to become the alpha I am, but at least you could put on the façade of one. I shouldn't even have to tell you this. You are my son. This should come to you like breathing."

Though everything in me wanted to buck against his system, I bared my neck in respect. "Yes, Alpha. I understand my duty."

"Well, blind obedience will do in the absence of true loyalty for the meantime. You need to make a decision while you are up there securing a future for yourself with this marriage. Dolrich is tough and commanding, unlike you. If not for me, he would've challenged you to a fight for the future seat as alpha already. I was giving you a chance to become what you were born to be. While you are taking this—" he flicked his hand in the air "—mate today, think about who it is that will take my place when I am gone. Think very hard if you want to give up on your legacy—the legacy of your family."

There was nothing to think about. The choice was already made.

CHAPTER 3

ATLAS

*T*he lace scratched my nose. If I wiggled my nose enough, maybe I would get my wish and teleport out of this place.

"Atlas Regina Belham, do you take the future alpha, Harrison Alphonso Xavier, to be your mate under the bear law?"

"Yes . . ." It sounded like a question.

A whisper in my ear frightened me. "I do is the proper response."

I cleared my throat. "I do."

I could've sworn I heard a chuckle across from me. He did *not* just laugh at me in front of what smelled and sounded like thousands of people. While his father, the alpha, was going on and on about something, my breath caught at the warmth of my hands. This male that was holding my hands, the one with whom I was damning myself to spend the next three months on some kind of probationary marriage, squeezed my hands. My brow scrunched in confusion. This was supposed to be cold and insincere. Yet, the gesture felt warm and almost soothing.

Plus, the man smelled like my favorite cake and my favorite waterfall mixed together.

Weird.

"Harrison Alphonso Xavier, do you take Atlas Regina Belham to be your mate under the bear law?"

"I do."

Of course, he didn't screw it up.

"By the power as Alpha of this kingdom, in front of our people, I proclaim you mates."

If this was normal, I would be able to see my mate—look into his eyes, feel the love in his words.

Hell, if this was normal, I would know what he looked like, for Creator's sake.

Also, there would be kissing.

Instead, we would be shuffled off to a room where we would strip ourselves of these blinders and see each other for the first time.

I didn't know which I wanted to do more, run or vomit.

"This way, ma'am." Someone put their hand in the crook of my arm, a female from the size and softness of the touch, and whispered in my ear when there was a step or when I was about to plow right into one of the guests. I felt like a toddler being led to time-out. She led me down what seemed like a hallway with no turns or stairs.

"Thank you?" My voice sounded weak.

"Yes. We all know you've come to help us. To help our kind. There are those who yell and shake their fists for war, but we know you are the key. You will free us from the alpha." As she went on, her tone grew faint. The scent of fear mingled with hope thickened the air around us.

"I will try."

Why did I say that? Here I was, blindfolded and wrapped in lace and pearls, pretending on one hand to be royalty and on the other, expected to be the rebel that set the captives free.

I had no idea how to be either.

A gentle pull on my elbow made me stop. A door opened, and I was ushered through.

"Here we are. Many blessings to the new couple. The alpha asks that you wait until I close the door before you remove your blindfolds. Thank you." It was a servant. I could tell from the hushed tones and careful steps. These royals had more servants than they did actual royalty.

I shouldn't talk.

I was one of them now.

It took what felt like hours for the door to shut. The click made my heartbeat race and my stomach pull taut with nervousness.

My mate's scent permeated the room. His smell was like the most subtle and pleasing cologne mixed with the richness of the forest trees. I was instantly intoxicated and humbled at once. I was in the room with—and mated to—a man who held my life like the strings on a puppet.

This man had the power to strike me from his sight in an instant.

Take back the payment on my parents' mortgage and all of my student loans.

More importantly, he had the power to take away this new relationship between the two classes. Never mind that he and his fellow royal asses wedged open the gap between the classes in the first place.

"Oh, thank you," the stranger muttered from behind me. I tried in vain not to let show the fact that his voice startled me. This man didn't need to think for a second that I scared easily.

And, of course they removed his first. He was the prince after all.

Two hands began to undo the ties on my blindfold, but halted almost as soon as they started. "No, it's fine. I will remove my bride's blindfold." He didn't even say thank you.

He just wanted to get his claws on me while we had a moment of privacy.

But mating completely wasn't in the deal. He could keep his royal paws to himself.

"Here you go." With fingers more nimble and gentle than I'd imagined, the binds to the blindfold were untied, and it fell to my feet. I took a moment to blink and steady my vision after so long in darkness.

"Thank you," I whispered. A shiver crawled down my spine as his breath fanned over the back of my neck. My body became frozen. The only thing I could do was stare ahead.

"Don't be scared. I promise I'm not all that ugly—just a little." His laughter blanketed my fear and forced me to turn around.

Ugly was the last word I would use for this man. It was strange. He was famous to us in a way that Banksy or someone just as elusive was. We knew all about him—where he went, the things he did. But we didn't know his face. Our people weren't allowed social media—the alpha's decree. Aside from the people in this castle, tucked away beyond a medieval veil, no one knew this man.

Until now.

"Hi," I said, way more breathless than I'd intended.

"Hello yourself, Atlas. That's a great name, by the way."

He smiled, and I had to forcefully stop myself from gasping. It lit up his entire face. For some reason, I thought a prince born in a castle would be softer. His features proved me wrong. A strong jawline and chiseled chin laid the foundation for a full mouth and eyes so dark and brown that I held my breath, thinking if I didn't, they might steal the air from me.

"Um, thank you. Harrison is pretty great, too."

He looked to the ground, as though he hadn't spent his entire life under an umbrella of praise.

"I'm not sure what we are supposed to do here. But I thought I might get some things out of the way."

"Shoot." *Damn it.* I sounded like I was from the block instead of a lady.

"Shoot. Okay. Just know that this wasn't my doing. I was commanded to take a female as a mate for political reasons. This isn't my idea of fun, and honestly, I was hoping to take a female for love one day. But, I suppose we should make the best of it. So let's be friends, okay?"

"Friends. That sounds great."

It sounded downright fantastic, actually. Except there was something about this man that all of a sudden made my insides melt, and I felt a blush rushing from my neck to my face faster than we'd tied the knot.

He extended his hand in my direction, and I took it, almost

thinking about offering him a fist bump. Something very 'lesser' of me to do.

I slid my hand into his, determined to make it as businesslike as possible.

Except his hand was soothingly hot, and as my fingers brushed his wrist, his other hand closed over mine, increasing the pressure and the warmth. One of his thumbs rubbed circles over the top of my hand, and subconsciously, I took a step toward him. When I looked up, eyes the color of dark chocolate blazed back at me, and when he smiled again, the force of his happiness tugged at the corners of those eyes, making them smile, too.

If I wasn't careful, I'd be lost.

"Ahem," I heard from the direction of the door, though I hadn't quite been able to take my eyes off of my newly mated male just yet to know who.

"I am Dolrich, Atlas." Someone was talking to me.

I'm sorry, the person you dialed is a puddle of goo right now. Try again later.

"Atlas, my cousin is trying to introduce himself. They probably also are requesting our presence at the party. Care to join us?"

My mate was now making fun of me.

Turning to face the new person in the room, I replied, "What? Oh, sorry. I was spaced out. It's very nice to meet you."

"You as well. Okay, couple of the year, let's get the party started. If you don't hurry, I'll be in trouble, and well, I'm in trouble all the time, so let's not get me another beating. Shall we?"

Dolrich was more charming than Harrison, but there was something boyish beneath the surface. His smile was so bright, it teetered on insincerity. His voice exuded self-confidence that bordered on vanity.

"Yes, of course. I apologize. It's been a long day." I took a moment to straighten my already straight dress and square off my shoulders, ready for the influx of royalty and lessers giving their hearty congratulations.

"No need to be formal around Harry and me, Atlas. But if the alpha is around, prim and proper, okay? You told her about the cursing, right? She looks like a girl who enjoys a good fuck once in a while. Shit, I meant *saying* fuck once in a while, not . . . Wow. Yeah, this is why I'm in trouble so much. Two minutes or my ass is grass."

He pointed to his watch and then shut the door behind him.

"What is this about cursing?"

"My dad hates it. Seriously, try like hell not to curse in front of him. He won't touch you, I can promise that, but let's not tempt fate. Ready? Or are you gonna zone out on me again?"

"I'm ready. Sorry. I just didn't expect you to be so . . ."

"Me, either." He laughed again, and it caused a thousand butterflies to come to life. "Me, either."

CHAPTER 4

HARRISON

*I*t took me a few seconds after she turned around before I could breathe right again.

They always told me that cinnamon bears were the lesser of our kind, but this woman, who was now my mate, was nothing lesser in my book.

I needed to know her better. The problem with getting to know her was that soon she would be gone, either by her own choice, or by me sending her away. She was a pawn in this game and didn't deserve to be included in the checkmate. It would be brutal when it all went down, one way or the other.

I might not have wanted this marriage, but I wouldn't see her hurt. With my hand on the small of her back, we listened to the congratulations all evening, and I purposefully steered her away from those who I knew opposed our marriage. They gave us death stares, especially Atlas, but I shielded her as best as I could from them when she was near me.

The split in the crowd was deep and obvious. Atlas spoke to the lesser, who were courteously invited, while I spoke to those I knew. The silly girl even took to having conversations with the servants who were also lessers. There were very few black bear servants among our employees. Further proof of the divide my father favored.

"Ladies and gentlemen, it is time for us to let the newly mated couple have their time together." My father's announcement wasn't embarrassing at all.

I caught a glance of Atlas's eyes growing wide. I glided through the crowd and pulled her closer, under my arm, in an attempt to calm her. She nodded slightly, and I took it to mean that it worked.

This wasn't fair to her, in this enormous marble-floored room with few others of her kind and her mother, who looked to have enjoyed the bar a little too much. She didn't even wish her daughter goodbye as my father announced our departure.

"Are you ready to go?" I asked her, bending to whisper in her ear.

"You have no idea," she said through a clenched jaw.

We waved and smiled like we were supposed to, but as soon as the doors to the great hall closed behind us, we both let out a loud and emotion-filled sigh.

Atlas spoke, still in a whisper. "Please tell me you have somewhere quieter to go. I think my eardrums are ready to burst."

"I have a whole wing to myself—to ourselves."

"Oh."

I grabbed her hand, and as fast as I could make my legs move, I took shortcuts and secret turns until we reached my side of the castle.

"We have the entire wing. Upstairs is the bedroom and downstairs is the semi-private common rooms. The servants won't come up here unless summoned. I can't say the same about my father. I want you to think of this place as your home while you are here. I'm assuming you have plans to stick this thing out for ninety days and then split." I led her into the bedroom. The furnishings were sparser than my father's side of the castle, but the level of luxury made me squirm. Even my platform bed was California king-sized, and the threads of gold weaved into the comforter were maddening. She would think that I was made of nothing but extravagance.

"Your clothes are in that closet over there. You have a separate bathroom. My mother set that up. We did some remodeling before you came. I'm not sure why she wants her own bathroom, but I imagine it's to get away from my father, but maybe she just likes some privacy. Now you can get away too." I laughed, but it wasn't sincere. My mother detested my father.

"I thought mates wanted to be together all the time," Atlas chimed in at my side now.

"True mates."

"Mates who are in love."

I corrected her. "Mates who are each half of the same person. Mates whose hearts are made for each other. Mates whose souls connect."

Why in the hell was I saying all of this? I sounded like a pathetic sap.

"Well, good thing you only have to put up with me for a while and then you can find that female. I'm sure she's out there."

"I don't even know how old you are, and yet I'm supposed to mark you tonight. Seems a little backwards."

"Well, we can fix that. You just have to mark me before the morning, right?"

"Right."

This time, my female took me by the hand and led me to the sofa, where she patted the place next to her.

"Hold on." I went into my closet and discarded the stiff tux, changing into a pair of gray sweatpants and a T-shirt with the logo of the Colorado Avalanche, my favorite hockey team.

When I walked back into the room, she squealed. "No fair. I'm stripping out of this lace-fest."

She stomped to her own closet and faster than I could've imagined, she returned, having changed into some black tight pants and a shirt that partially exposed her right shoulder.

She was too tempting for her own good.

"Better?" I asked as she plopped down beside me, pulling her feet under her legs with one swift movement. It was like she was in her element again.

"Can I say something?" Atlas blurted as my mouth opened to begin our mini-interrogation.

"Of course."

She scooted closer and leaned forward, her eyes on my lips. Waves of warmth were trailing from her to me so intensely that I held my breath.

"I'm starving. Please tell me there's a kitchen in this place. For shifters, you people sure don't eat much."

A laugh burst from my mouth before I could stop it. It sounded like me—a me I hadn't heard in years.

"Of course. I have a magic phone and everything. What's your poison?" I reached for the phone behind the sofa and dialed the kitchen. "Yo, Oscar, hook us up with some snacks. My female is hungry."

CHAPTER 5

ATLAS

I was stalling. Big time.

I no more wanted this male to bite me on the shoulder than I wanted to get my period six times a month.

Actually, I really was hungry. There were snotty little hoity-toity hors d'oeuvres at the party, but they weren't enough to fill up a turtle.

Harrison listened for a few minutes and then agreed with whatever Oscar was saying.

"Sorry, Oscar likes to talk hockey. Even on my wedding night, apparently. The food will be here in a few minutes. Anything else you need? I'm being a bad host."

"Nope. Let's get this started. Since you and your cousin started the conversation . . . first curse word and how old?"

He leaned back and thought a while. "Eight or nine, I think, and it was 'ass'. That's my mom's favorite word."

I thought back over the events of the day. I hadn't spoken to Harrison's mother all night. Speaking to Harrison's mother was something I actually looked forward to. She was said to be a lovely, kind, and generous queen.

The alpha queen was the one person in this household whom my people did not completely despise. Harrison had better not expect me to sit in a corner and not speak to anyone like some kind of blind and deaf trophy wife.

Shit, I guess I would have to if I wanted our debt paid and a life that would be money-worry free.

"I didn't get a chance to talk to her tonight."

"Who, my mom? Did you want to?"

I shrugged. "I've heard a lot about her. She seems like good people."

"My mother is the best of people. Some days she's the only reason I don't run like hell from this place."

"Like you could even get out of here."

He gave me some serious side-eye. "Maybe I can."

I was about to ask him what he meant and where the door was to get there when a light knock at his—or our—bedroom door sounded, and in walked a strong-looking young man, maybe a few years younger than Harrison and me. Maybe he was the same age as both of us. I would add that question to the list of the many things I didn't know about the man I had just married.

"Everything you ordered and a few things for the lady," he said, a little more joyfully than I would expect from a servant. "Enjoy your evening."

He set down a large tray of delicious smelling food and left before I managed to get a thank you out.

"We played as children. He was the only other kid in the castle. It's weird to call on him for things now. But I'm glad he got to stay."

Whatever the memory was that Harrison was thinking about made him look downcast.

"Were you lonely as a child?"

He shrugged and took the lids off several silver platters full of a tailgater's dream spread. "What about you? I'm tired of talking about me. Do you have brothers and sisters? They told me nothing about you other than you were educated and beautiful. They were correct on that account, by the way."

"I have four brothers, all older. They weren't allowed to come tonight."

His shoulders fell as he picked up an empty plate and selected one of each item. "I'm sorry. I don't make the rules. You said you were hungry?"

He held the plate out to me, and I was so taken aback, it took me a few seconds to react. When I did, our hands brushed, and the feeling of warmth from before came back with a fury.

But this time the sensation reverberated all over my body.

"Do you feel that, or is it just me?"

He looked stricken. "I thought it was just me. It must be because you are new here or something. We have to go to the Court of the Sun and the Moon to get your tattoo tomorrow. Maybe after that, everything will be normal again. It might be the only chance for us to get out of the castle grounds for a while, so enjoy it."

From the tone of his voice, normal wasn't something he wanted.

"So, tell me about this place. I mean, there are rumors, but I was blindfolded from the time I stepped off the airplane until I got to the room in the castle where my dress was. It was kind of ridiculous."

He sat next to me. I noticed he didn't make himself a plate. "There's too much to tell you tonight, but I can tell you some. Havenwood Falls was founded in the 1800s by a few families who were fleeing persecution. They were attracted to this place because of the location, and they swear there's something magical about the falls."

He spouted the history like a teacher lecturing students, like he had no attachment to it.

"Your family was one of those?"

"No. We came a few years later. It's a point of contention with my father. That might be a subject to avoid in conversation with him."

The alpha from my clan back home in Louisiana was apparently very different from Harrison's father. Black bears had one alpha over all clans, which was Harrison's father. Then each smaller clan had their own alpha. Ours was Kar. He was the leader of a big family. We didn't walk on eggshells around him. He was kind, just, and fair to all bears, and he certainly didn't see my lighter hair as anything lesser.

He was one of us.

No wonder these people needed a bridge to the real world.

"Maybe you can take me into town someday." Harrison looked uncomfortable again. "What?"

"We aren't encouraged to leave the castle or the grounds. We are protected by a separate veil than even Havenwood Falls. The town is protected by a ward to keep the supes around here protected, but that wasn't enough for the alpha. My father is constantly paranoid that the mages from the Luna Coven are out to get us. So he had a mage from Romania, who is not tied to the Luna Coven, come in and guard the castle with new veils."

If I had a bunch of balloons, he would've just popped all of them with one stick. When I looked back up, my new mate was studying me. His gaze made me nervous again.

Harrison smiled. "Good thing I wasn't a very well-behaved child."

I couldn't imagine a naughty bone in this prince's body, but I perked up at the notion of getting out of this stuffy place just hours after arriving.

"Can we go to the falls?" I was a little eager already.

"I know a way. But first, we have to get your tattoo. It will protect you from hunters and make you recognizable to other shifters. And there are other things we have to take care of before we can even think about sneaking you out of the castle. Like . . . the mate marking."

I knew the conversation was coming, I just hoped to avoid it for . . . forever.

"Do we have to do that tonight?"

CHAPTER 6

HARRISON

I swallowed against the thought that she didn't want to proceed with the marking. "We do. Trust me. There will be people tomorrow morning who will not only notice, but will be looking for the mark. It's our first test, of sorts."

Atlas twisted a piece of her long brown hair around her pointer finger.

"What if this doesn't work out?"

I took a long, deep breath and stood up to stretch my legs. "Good. I'm glad we're on the same page."

She stood up as well. "Same page?"

"You obviously aren't planning on letting this mating go any further than it has to. Is that right? You're just here to make the ninety days and then go back to your life, money in hand?" The tone of my voice reminded me of my father in the worst way possible. I paused at the callousness of my own words and shook my head. "I'm sorry. That was wrong to say. It's been a long day. We haven't even been mated for a few hours, and I'm being an asshole."

She didn't answer at first. Before long, her slim hand ran over the top of my shoulder, and I shivered at her touch. "Look, this is hard," she finally said. "Let's not pretend it's not. As long as we are honest with each other, we can get through this. Right?"

I kind of liked this woman already. This wasn't the plan.

"You want honesty? Okay. My father will be looking for the mark tomorrow morning. I don't even want to think about what will happen if you don't have it, and I don't want anything to happen to you."

There was so much truth to that last sentence. I'd just met this female, and yet something gnawed at me to protect her from my father, like I'd always protected my mother to the best of my ability.

"Well, we have to keep the alpha happy, right? Are you ready?" She looked around the room. For what, I had no idea. "The bed would be appropriate, right? Although, we don't want to get blood on the comforter. Prince's choice."

Atlas calling me Prince was like running fingernails down a chalkboard. It made my jaw clench.

"Harrison, please. Let's not call me Prince. Unless you want me to sing. I do a mean Purple Rain."

She tried, in vain, to quell a smile. "You know, I think I knew that about you already, somehow."

"There's a ton you don't know about me. And probably a hell of a lot more that I don't know about you."

Atlas grabbed my hand and led me toward the window seat, a place that I'd never really sat. I knew it was there; it just seemed impractical.

"So who goes first?" she said, and a touch of a blush came over her face.

I cleared my throat. The moonlight filtered through the slivers between the sheer curtains, making sparkles dance on her already shiny brown hair and causing her skin to glow with an ethereal opalescence.

My father had chosen well.

"I don't think it matters. Maybe I should." With one swift movement, I was next to her. Our knees and legs met, and my face was inches from hers. She sucked in a breath, and this close, I could hear her heart racing and tripping over skipped beats. "I'll make this as painless as possible."

She nodded, and I hoped it was because she was as breathless as I was.

"I, Harrison, mark you, Atlas, as my mate and future queen of the black bear shifters. You shall always be protected, taken care of, and nurtured as long as you are my mate."

I made up the last sentence.

I pulled her shirt to the side, exposing her right shoulder. The pulse on her neck grew frantic. My hand trailed from her ear down the curve of her throat before cupping her fair shoulder. My other hand slid behind her neck, threading my fingers in her hair, mostly because I needed to know how it felt, but a little to keep her in place so she didn't struggle against the pressure.

I counted to three under my breath and then marked my mate.

CHAPTER 7

ATLAS

I tried like hell to be brave, and I was, until his hand ran down the length of my neck. Then there was no point in pretending. I was scared as fuck. Not of the bite or of the pain. I feared this male in front of me. The way his voice blanketed my senses scared me. The way his brown eyes bored directly into mine whenever he spoke made me anxious. Whenever he touched me, my insides burned with a desire I'd never felt, and I feared I never would again.

This can't be happening.

The moment his teeth grazed my skin, I let out a wail that was a concoction of pain and complete and utter passion. Euphoria and pleasure shot through my shoulder and didn't waste any time reaching the rest of my body. He was there, with me, a part of me, sucking and drinking my blood, my life source, and connecting us in a way that I'd been naive enough to think wasn't intimate, wasn't inflaming, wasn't somehow permanent.

When his arms moved around me, my body gave in to all the sensations, and I allowed them. I sunk into his hold like molten metal flows into a mold.

My body in his arms was absolute perfection.

When he pulled back, I groaned at the loss.

"That was . . ." he started, but couldn't finish.

I nodded, still unable to form a coherent sentence.

"Hold on." He stood up, and I slumped against the window, still feeling like goo. "Let's get that cleaned up. I'm sorry. I probably took more than I should've. We can wait a few minutes before we . . ."

He didn't get to finish his sentence. With a new surge of energy, I reached out, fueled purely by instinct, and pulled him down to me. There was barely enough time to pull his T-shirt away from his shoulder. "I, Atlas, take you, Harrison, as my mate and mark you now."

They weren't the right words, but in that pulsing moment, I didn't fucking care. I needed him, then and there.

A moan poured from his lips as my teeth pierced his flesh. A burst of warmth hit my tongue as his decadent blood cascaded into my mouth. Sammy had said something to me once, in shifter class, that royal blood was rumored to taste different, but I wasn't prepared for the richness flowing down my throat in waves of connection.

"Atlas?" Harrison's voice broke through my haze and back into reality.

"Oh!" I jerked back and gasped. "I'm sorry. I don't know what happened."

"It's okay. I just want to make sure I have as much energy as possible for tomorrow morning."

As he'd just explained, I knew I'd be going to the Court the next day to get my tattoo, but other than that, I hadn't planned on running a marathon.

"What's tomorrow?"

He ran a finger lazily down the side of my face, looking absolutely uncaring about the blood seeping through his shirt. "Tomorrow I start protecting you from my father and, I suspect, keeping you out of trouble. You're going to cause me trouble, aren't you?"

I shrugged. Wasn't that my goal in this arrangement? To cause as much trouble as possible for this pampered prince, so that by the end of the ninety days, or even before that, he would toss me out along with the other lessers they found so easily expendable.

That was still my goal.

Harrison's face fell a little when I didn't react to his lure. I would have to guard myself against this prince. I'd already given him too much. Too much of my laughter. Too many of my smiles.

Less than a day in this forsaken palace, and I'd lost who I was.

Lost in his eyes. Caressed by his hands. Drunk on his blood.

Fuck.

"I'm going to take a shower." A coldness came over me as he walked toward the bathroom.

No, it was just my imagination. I couldn't possibly be cold just because Harrison Xavier wasn't near me.

CHAPTER 8

HARRISON

We'd slept in the same bed, but hadn't touched the entire night. The rope that tied us together through our mating marks had thinned during the night, as though we were both tugging our bond in opposite directions.

It was too weak to not fray in the middle.

Atlas was awake. Her breaths were steady, but purposefully shallow. She'd taken a bath after my shower. Her hair, straight on the day of our mating, was now in waves and absolutely everywhere on the bed. The strands of cinnamon brown were a stark contrast to the gold of the silk sheets around her.

"Good morning," I said softly. There was no time for her to answer. A knock at the door jolted us both out of bed. Already nervous about who was on the other side of the door, I put my hands on her shoulders. She winced in pain.

"I'm sorry. I forgot. That might be my father." The fear and desperation for her to survive every encounter with my father made me sound weak. I hated to be weak in front of this female. "It's going to be okay."

She looked at me, sleepy crinkles still at the corners of her eyes. "Is he going to eat us?"

I laughed. She made me laugh at the weirdest times. "No."

"Bring it."

Trouble. The female was trouble.

"Come in." I tried to yell, but it sounded more goat than self-confident prince of a kingdom.

I heard his footsteps and smelled his overbearing cologne before the servant cleared the way for his entrance. Leave it to my father to risk interrupting an intimate moment between a newly mated couple, and think it was perfectly okay.

My father strolled into the bedroom. His gaze moved around the room. He'd expressed some discontent about my sparse furnishings, but I liked my side of the castle simple and less gaudy than his. Even my mother had confessed a gag reflex in regard to her side of the castle and all the gold trimmings it held. After his appraisal of the room, he zeroed in on Atlas, now my marked mate, still waking up.

"Neck," I seethed at Atlas.

We both tilted our heads and bared our necks, showing respect. Atlas reached out and took my hand, but there was no fear in her smell.

One of my father's eyebrows rose. "I see the little couple are up bright and early."

Like he gave us a choice.

"Good morning, Alpha." Atlas spoke first, and I suppressed the need to cover her mouth with my hand so that there were no repercussions from my father. She had no idea what he could do— what he had done.

"Good morning, little cinnamon princess." There wasn't a lick of sarcasm in his tone. "I see you two have gotten along quite well on the night of your mating."

My bear nearly clawed his way through my chest at the sight of my father's hand on her shoulder where my mark was. He knew it, too. The alpha's black eyes shifted to mine in an unspoken dare for me to say something to him about it.

"We have, Alpha. I'm so grateful for your kindness and for choosing me as your son's mate." Damn, she was good.

"We are thankful to have you here, Atlas. Well, I am satisfied that things are going as planned. The Court of the Sun and the Moon are awaiting you this morning. As you know, all supernatural beings must report to them. They think highly of themselves, especially that supposed representative of the shifters, Ulrich Kasun." My father spat Ric's name.

"Of course, Alpha."

He turned to leave. "Good job, Harrison. I had my doubts."

Those were his last words before leaving.

Atlas stood in silence, still holding my hand while she waited, for what I had no clue. "And I thought *we* were supposed to be the lessers."

"What?" The word choked out.

"Seriously, you guys are so pampered and proper, but at the same time, completely passive-aggressive and rude. I'd rather stick a screwdriver in my head than ever speak to that man again."

"You guys?" I asked, attempting to veil the knife in my back.

"I guess not you. You know what I mean."

I stepped closer to her, grabbing her other hand. "I've tried all my life not to be like those people, Atlas. One day you will see that in me."

"What do I need to wear for the Court?" She changed the subject.

"Not completely casual, but not anything too dressy. Just whatever."

CHAPTER 9

ATLAS

*T*he alpha gave me the creeps more than I was afraid of him. The way he touched my shoulder was a little too intimate— a little too personal.

I shrugged on an emerald green dress and black stilettos before taming my wild, golden brown locks. I wanted them out and free. The royal hair-people had tied it all up for the mating ceremony, as though they were trying to hide my cinnamon.

I was letting my cinnamon shine.

I came out, and our bedroom was already being cleaned by three servants, all cinnamon. For a moment, meeting each of their eyes, I felt like a traitor.

My mate assessed my outfit. "You look . . . Are you ready to go?"

Harrison wore gray pants with a lighter gray button-down shirt. His stubble had already started to grow into a beard, and it took all there was in me not to reach out and touch it for myself.

I had to stay the course.

This was only temporary.

"Yes. I'm ready."

We went downstairs and entered a car that cost more than all my student loans combined. The alpha and his wife were in the car ahead of us, and I had yet to meet my mother-in-law. This place was absolutely ridiculous.

"Want to give me some background? What am I walking into?"

"Nothing that's a big deal. You have to introduce yourself to the Court, because you are now future royalty, and then get your tattoo. Ric Kasun, the seat holder on the Court, will officially introduce you. The rest is formalities."

It was the formalities that scared me the most.

"Who is Ric Kasun?"

Harrison looked out the windshield before speaking. He reached between us and pushed a button that made the privacy screen rise between us and the driver. It was like a movie or something. And also ridiculous.

"Ric Kasun is the head of the Kasun pack of wolves. My father and he are like two rabid dogs when they see each other. Dad thinks the seat on the Court should be ours, and Ric hates my father and thinks he's a pompous ass. Ric would be right, by the way. But, in public, it would be wise of us to be on my father's side of things. Ric may be right, but we have to live in the castle with my father. You know?"

"Know where your bread is buttered."

"What?"

"My mom says that. Know where your bread is buttered."

Harrison laughed again, and damn it all if somehow the sound didn't penetrate my chest and make my heart beat double time.

Without warning, he scooted over in the car and pulled me against his side. He was warm, warmer than anyone I knew. "Please don't make me do anything against the alpha to protect you. Don't make me choose, because after last night, I will choose you, and we know what will happen if you aren't the new alpha's queen. You do know, don't you?"

I did. It was all under the guise of a pretty package and a lovely little wedding, but the fact was, I was the bargaining chip for the lessers, the cinnamon bears. They were at their wits' end from being treated like second-class citizens, and well, lesser than the black bears. We were technically all the same species, just a different color than the rest. The cinnamon bears were pushed aside and forced into servant positions, cleaning the alpha's floors.

I was the only thing preventing an all-out revolution. "I do. I don't want my people killed."

"All of our people. I don't want any of our people killed, cinnamon or black. I want us all united, like we used to be."

"Before the Xaviers took leadership."

He nodded, and his ear brushed mine as he did. "Took is the right word."

I pulled back with a jerk and looked him in the eye. There was no lie on his tongue. We bear shifters could taste a lie from a great distance, even the hint of untruth.

"You'll have to tell me about that one day."

He nodded again. "Let me begin the conversation when we do. Trust me. Some of the castle walls listen and talk. I know the safe places."

I could hear my heart beating between my temples and in my ears. There were too many things happening beneath the surface of all this water.

I opened my mouth to ask more questions, but the car halted and the doors opened. A Cheshire grin pulled at the corners of the alpha's face as he saw Harrison and me so close. To him, it probably looked like a successful coupling on his part.

"We are here. Harrison, I trust you've briefed your mate of the situation with these . . . these beings. We do what they say, but they get nothing more."

Harrison nodded and opened the door further to get out before me, strategically placing himself between me and his father. "Of course, Alpha. My mate is ready for this. Aren't you, Atlas?"

It was time for me to pretend to be the meek little female again. *Ick*.

"Yes, Alpha. Harrison has made sure I know all I need to."

That was a little much, even for me.

"Good. Let's get this over with. My bear is itching to burst out and claw those wolves already, and we haven't even gotten in the door."

Alphas were supposed to be steady and still and responsive instead of reactive, yet this man was the very opposite. The scent of his restlessness hung in the air.

A woman came through the doorway and approached us, her hands outstretched and a smile gleaming on her face. Her silvery, almost snowy, hair was pulled up in a chignon. An air of regality flowed about her.

"That's Saundra Beaumont," Harrison whispered into my ear.

We walked toward her, and I noticed Harrison's mother wasn't coming.

"Your mother isn't joining us?" I thought about it for a second, trying like hell to be as diplomatic as possible. "I'd love for another female bear to be with me for the tattoo."

Our company stopped, and I knew I'd done it. One day in, and I'd done poked the bear—literally.

Saundra replied, "Actually, that is an excellent idea. Divine, won't you come and join your new daughter-in-law in receiving her new marking?"

Harrison's mom looked like someone just gave her the biggest brownie she'd ever seen. Practically running, she looped her arm in mine and gave it a squeeze.

If I were ever to be queen, she would be treated like she deserved.

I'm not sure what I thought the Court of the Sun and the Moon would look like, but it seemed somehow less formal and more bustling in friendly conversation.

"Welcome to the Court, young bear, future queen of the Black Bears."

I didn't know who the woman was, but she seemed to be the leader.

"Thank you," I answered with a smile.

"We have already approved you to stay in Havenwood Falls, of course, but there is the question of the tattoo."

Harrison stepped forward. "The tattoo, Saundra?"

Saundra. That was her name.

"Yes. She can have an invisible mark or a visible one. One

matching her mate's or another one. It is her choice, and her choice alone."

The alpha stiffened beside us. Apparently, he didn't like anyone having a choice about anything.

"Give us one moment, Saundra, please."

The woman nodded once.

Harrison pulled me to him, placing his hand on my waist. "It really is your choice. It's your body."

"What is yours?" My whisper wasn't much quieter than a regular tone, so there were several snickers around the room from those who heard me.

"A bear. Visible."

I cleared my throat and decided to thoroughly embarrass myself. "Can I get one that is only visible to my mate, but other shifters can see another tattoo?"

To my surprise, there was no more laughter.

Saundra paused and then nodded. "You may. I've never heard of it before, but I like the idea. Emilian, I like this new daughter-in-law of yours. She brings new ideas and hope to Havenwood Falls."

Too bad the alpha didn't strike me as one who appreciated new ideas.

Saundra extended her hand to me and my mother-in-law. "Let's begin, then. Divine, are you accompanying your new daughter?"

The alpha queen nodded and curled her long black hair over her shoulder.

"It shall be done."

CHAPTER 10

HARRISON

J wasn't sure how long my tattoo had taken. I was just a child. But it had to be a shorter time period than three hours. That, coupled with my father's incessant pacing and the random checks to make sure the door that my mate went behind was still locked, told me it was taking longer than anyone expected.

"What is taking so long, wolf?" Our alpha's question was directed to the Kasun pack's alpha, who didn't look distressed in the slightest.

"I'm not sure, Emilian. In a hurry?"

My dad hated the Kasun clan more than he hated most other supernaturals in Havenwood Falls, and that was saying something. Though I'd never heard my father specifically say anything to support the theory, I thought that maybe he had been running from someone or something when he decided to come to Havenwood Falls. I knew that his father had been run out of several other places for his rigidity and callous rule over the bears, but he had never been replaced.

Also, my father hated humans in general, and Havenwood Falls seemed like a place he could avoid them.

"We have business to attend to. I'm sure my son would like to have his mate back as well."

Just as I thought I might have to step in between the two of them and completely embarrass myself, the three women came through the door.

They were . . . embracing.

My father would not be pleased.

"What is this, a tattooing or girls' night out? Let's go now."

Saundra whispered something into Atlas's ear that caused her to stroke her newly inked neck. I tried to make out what the tattoo was, but she pulled on her coat, and my chance was gone.

Hopefully, she would give me another chance to see it.

Outside City Hall, through the door marked with the mountain and moon, my father clenched and unclenched his fists all the way to the car before he turned on us with a smirk.

"Made friends, did we, Divine?"

He spoke to my mother, called her by name, but his eyes were targeted on Atlas. I knew that look. My father was about to attempt one of his passive-aggressive lessons.

"Saundra has known us since we came to Havenwood Falls, my dear. Of course we are friends. And I was so honored to be with Atlas during her tattoo. It was a chance for me to bond with my daughter-in-law."

"Those people hate us. They don't approve of us, and if it were up to them, the humans that visit this town would walk right up to the castle's front door to greet us, along with those lessers."

Fuck it all. I thought with Atlas as my mate, he would at least have the decency to keep his lesser bear hate concealed.

My father's paranoia about the Court was his own, and not even close to the truth. The Court would never expose our castle to humans. They wouldn't want any humans to discover any of the supernatural powers in this place. It would destroy everything they'd worked to protect.

Atlas blurted, "Why don't we leave this place then, Alpha? The tattoo is done. There is no need for me or any of us to be around these people any longer. Don't you agree, Harrison?"

I was almost speechless. Plus, I was a little frustrated. Didn't she know she was going to get herself in trouble?

"I agree. Father, I'd like very much to get my mate back home again."

"Let's go. I also want to get my female home. Get the stench of the Court from her skin."

There was no stench. Saundra simply smelled like magic. My father was being overly dramatic about a feud that I knew was solely in his mind.

As soon as the door closed on the car, Atlas started speaking. I didn't let her finish.

"No, Atlas. Didn't you listen to me? You don't understand his temper. You don't understand what he could do. What if he hurt you? What if he took you away?"

Fuck, I sounded too desperate.

I couldn't help myself. After biting her, having her life force in my body, there had to be a change of plans. Even if I was never to be alpha, she had to remain mine.

"Fine. I'll try. That's all I can promise. So we're stuck in the castle again?"

"For a time. Until my father goes out of town in the morning. Then we can roam. The people of Havenwood Falls, well, the supernatural ones, don't tell my father or his spies when they see me in town. They will keep us safe."

Atlas was looking out the window, still with her collar pulled up. I was dying to see her marking.

She stayed still and silent the rest of the ride home.

"Wait!" she said before we exited the car.

"What?" I actually looked her up and down like an idiot to see what was wrong with her.

"Can we have some kind of signal? Like you can signal me when it's okay for me to be myself?"

That was actually smart and would help me keep her safe.

She continued, "What if you touch your nose or something?"

"I never touch my nose. My father would notice. What if I just held your hand? Squeezed when we are safe, when you are safe."

I took her hand and squeezed to show her.

She blushed before whispering, "That's good."

We got out of the car, and she didn't let go.

CHAPTER 11

ATLAS

*A*fter we returned to the castle, Harrison was summoned to some kind of briefing. He left me in the library, which contained thousands of books that looked to have never been touched.

A clearing throat caught my attention and drew my eyes across the monstrous room, where all the walls not filled with books were lined with aged maple.

"Hello?"

The male stepped forward. It was Oscar, from the night before.

"Atlas, can we speak for a moment?"

"Of course." I looked around for his sake, making sure the alpha wasn't hanging from the ceiling or something.

"Not here." With two fingers, he waved me toward the door. I smelled no deception on him, so I followed. Oscar stopped at the entrance of a closet that was the size of my old apartment. "In here."

I stepped inside, thinking that I would find brooms or mops, but instead I found a makeshift living area with a few chairs and a shabby table.

"I apologize. There aren't very many places that are safe here."

"It's fine. What did you need to talk to me about?"

"I wanted to warn you about some things and to ask your intentions. Everyone is getting their hopes up, but I'm the skeptic."

He sat down once I did, and I motioned for him to continue. My heart jumped into my throat in anticipation.

"The warning is about saying anything in certain places of the house. There are very few places that are safe. I'm sure Harrison will tell you. The other is that not everything is what it seems here. Look beyond the mask. Don't trust anyone."

"Even you?" I said, with my eyebrow cocked.

"You can trust your kind, Atlas. We would never betray you. I wanted to invite you to a place where you can see what's really going on here."

"And where is that?"

"The Terrace. Just ask your mate. He will know where it is, though he has never been. Don't be surprised if he bucks against the idea. He's been brainwashed too long."

"Brainwashed?"

He ticked his head to the right and stared down the door. He heard something.

"Back to the library, Atlas. Quickly. You know the way?"

Oscar pushed me out the door, not waiting for the answer. I looked both ways down the hall and spotted a painting I'd remembered passing.

The castle was a maze, but I feared that getting lost in this place was the least of my worries.

THE WALLS of stone seemed to close in minute by minute. Harrison's father didn't leave the next day or the next. We spent our time in an endless schedule of increasingly boring blocks of time.

You can learn a lot about someone when you're confined in a space with them. My mate was kind, but at the same time aloof to the staff. This might have been because he'd been taught to act this way, or maybe it was his father's disposition coming through.

He was also oblivious. He was like a child playing in a playpen while the world burned around him. He wasn't doing anything about it, but at the same time I wondered if he even knew the severity of the world outside.

I would have to show him before he became alpha and turned into his father.

That was, if I didn't die of boredom first.

I even played chess with my mate just to pass the time.

He didn't seem to notice my little spurts of time away from him. Either that, or he didn't care. The servants of the castle were more than willing to divulge information to me, since I was one of their kind. I'd snuck to the kitchen and even the laundry rooms to speak to them.

My mate was ignorant on so many levels.

A knock on the library door startled me. Jerking out of my chair, I rose to answer the door, knocking over all the pieces except Harrison's king.

"Let the servants answer the door," Harrison whispered to me. I'd come to know this whisper as the 'helping Atlas stay out of trouble' whisper. The things he told me to do in this whisper were not meant as commands, but precautions.

I'd always been pretty independent before, but having Harrison keep me safe didn't bother me.

In fact, I kind of found it endearing.

"Ah, here is the happy couple. Your mother and I are going to meet with some of the clans in the west. We will be gone for just a couple of days. Dolrich will be coming with me."

Waiting for Harrison to have some kind of reaction to his father taking a cousin with him on a trip for official business, I stayed quiet. Not calm, but quiet.

I looked back and forth between father and son, waiting for a protest or at least a flash of disgruntled emotions, but there were none. Apparently, both of them were content with the status quo.

"Excellent. Are there any tasks you would have me do while you are gone?" Harrison sounded like the girl from Rohan in Lord of the Rings, all prim and proper about official duties.

"No. I have everything taken care of. You and Atlas just . . . do whatever you do."

There was a hint of perversion when the alpha referred to me and his son. Every. Time.

Harrison nodded. At first, I thought he was afraid of his father, but more and more, I believed it to be tolerance.

It was as if Harrison just didn't care. What kind of future leader would he be if he didn't care about the kingdom—just let it all swirl around him while he sat on his chairs and walked in his libraries and ordered food from the phone?

Twenty minutes later, the car with the alpha and his queen pulled from the driveway.

We both watched from the window of the library, directly above the main entrance to the castle.

"When can we . . ."

Harrison gasped slightly. It wasn't safe for me to speak. I'd forgotten. It was like living under a dictator instead of an honorable leader.

I'd have bet Harrison would be an honorable leader if he was given the right opportunity. We waited in the library another half hour. My legs nervously bounced the entire time, mostly because I knew we were waiting for a sign of the alpha being gone.

The sign that we could leave this place.

"Why don't we go take a walk in the gardens?" Harrison asked, already almost halfway to the door.

"Okay." This place was so weird.

We strolled through the maze of flowers and trees. There were shrubs shaped into beings and animals, Edward Scissorhands style, and roses whose blooms were twice the size of any blooms I'd ever seen.

"Yeah?" Harrison lifted his cell to his ear. I hadn't even heard a ring.

"Good. Thank you, Ric."

"Ric?" I asked in total confusion. There had to be another Ric.

"Yeah, that Ric. My father keeps enemies. I keep friends. Sorry, I forgot the hand thing." He took my hand and squeezed. "This garden is always safe if you need to come out and scream or tell me something or you know, drag your mate out here to make out." He laughed and shrugged. Not even sorry for tempting me.

All of a sudden, I was in some kind of bear soap opera.

"So I can trust Ric, too? If I needed something?"

His expression grew serious. "If you need anything or find yourself in a situation out in the Falls, you can go to any member of the Court of the Sun and the Moon. They are all allies, so to speak. As my mate, you will be protected."

"And as the future queen?"

"Maybe it's time for you to show me your ink." He was changing the subject. Fine with me. I didn't really want to talk about being the queen anyway.

"Oh. Here." I pulled at the collared button-down shirt, one of many that my mother insisted I bring. She mistook a castle for a preppy private school.

"It's a bear, no, it's two bears. One looks like mine."

I shrugged. "They might as well know who I belong . . . who my mate is."

He moved in closer. I could feel the rhythm of his breaths against my neck. "I thought it would look different to me than it does to everyone else."

My blush rose to my cheeks, putting the red roses around me to shame. "Um, if the mating is ever completed, it will change to something else that only you can see."

Harrison's eyes grew to large circles. "Oh, that must've been what took so long. Addie must've used a good bit of magic."

"She did. She had some predictions about us."

"Oh?" He cleared his throat. "What were they? We are safe here." He must've seen my apprehension.

"That we would change this clan. Actually, she said we would change the future of all bears. There was more, but it was . . ."

"Was what?" He took another step toward me. His warm hand brushed mine, sending tingles down my spine and making my stomach pull tight. The scent of my mate overwhelmed me when he got this close. It was all I could do not to pretend this was all real and let myself fall for him.

"Nothing. Just that we would have a lot of children." The words spilled from my mouth faster and sloppier than I'd ever spoken before.

He said nothing, so I stole a glance at him, still standing too close.

He winked at me. "Sounds like fun. Let me know when you want to get started on that." With a kiss to my new tattoo, he left me there, panting.

CHAPTER 12

HARRISON

"*A*re you coming with me? I thought you wanted to see the falls. We might not have another chance."

"Where are we going?"

I looked over my shoulder. With arms crossed over her chest, she pretended to want to defy me—not to follow me.

"The falls. Isn't that where you wanted to go? You know, our kind say that a couple who visits the falls together will never be parted in this life. They will fall in love if they aren't already. Get it? Fall at the falls?" I sounded like an idiot again.

"Wow. That was horrible. You get girls with those lines?"

It didn't matter how awful the joke was, it got her feet moving toward me. I held out my hand for her, not to signal anything, just to be able to touch her again.

Her soft fingers laced through mine.

"Looks like I got one girl with that line."

"Maybe."

We walked to the edge of the gardens, where an unassuming shed stood.

"Um, Harrison? This is creepy."

"It's our transportation."

A scoffing sound came from my mate.

"It's a motorcycle. Calm down. I told you, when my father is gone, we are free."

Somewhere in the conversation, she'd let go of my hand. But she took it again before she spoke. "Don't you think we should all be free even when your father is here? You are the future heir to the throne, Harrison, and even you feel imprisoned. Imagine how my people feel. Yes, they smile when they bring our tea. Yes, they are polite when they come to collect the laundry. But they are not free—just like you and me right now. What if your father decides to turn the plane around and come back? Will you pale and have to bring us home to pretend to play chess?"

The world stopped turning for me.

"I'm sorry. There's nothing I can do until I become alpha, *if* I become alpha."

"What? What do you mean?"

Shit. I had to tell Atlas about my plans soon. She could be an ally for me.

Some servants had come out to prune the roses at the most inopportune time. Even in my garden, there were spies that pretended to be gardeners. They'd never come out when I was there before. By the coal color of their hair and the same colored eyes, I knew they were black bears, not cinnamon like the other servants. They weren't gardeners at all.

"Now this place isn't safe. Let's go take a drive. Come on."

I unlocked the padlock on the door and jumped onto the motorcycle, kicking up the stand with my heel.

"What?" I asked. She was still in the doorway, not looking pleased.

"That's dangerous."

Taking Atlas to a secluded place while she was so damned tempting—that was dangerous. "It's fine. I ride it all the time. Trust me?"

CHAPTER 13

ATLAS

*T*ruth be told, I hadn't quite arrived at the word trust when it came to Harrison. Lust? Yes. Attraction? Yes. Respect? Yes. Trust?

"Almost." Honesty was the best policy, right?

For a moment, I thought maybe I'd hurt him. My chest throbbed with a huffing sound I didn't recognize as my own.

"Is that you making that sound? Your bear?" I asked, rubbing my chest with my fist. I hadn't meant to ask the question out loud. It was well known that bears made a similar sound while in the presence of their mate. Except, I hadn't expected it with Harrison. He was still little more than a stranger to me in most ways.

"I think so. Must be a mates thing. Is it almost enough to get on and go with me?"

I thought about it for a second. More than trusting Harrison, I wanted to see Havenwood Falls, the place, not the town. I wanted to see what this mecca of sorts was about. Saundra had talked about it like unicorns and fairies lived there in their spare time.

In seconds, I was on the motorcycle, strapping on a helmet, rendering an answer unnecessary. Harrison reached behind him and circled my arms around his waist, patting my hands. I'd never been on a motorcycle. It seemed reckless.

Then again, everything in my life lately was reckless.

Beyond the grounds of the castle, my vision got blurry. Trees appeared and reappeared. We were passing the same landmarks over and over. My mate had successfully gotten us lost. I patted his stomach to get his attention, trying not to think about the vicinity of my hands.

"What?" he yelled.

"You're lost. We are lost."

He chuckled, and his stomach moved with it under my hands. "We're not. Hang tight."

Two more turns that almost made my breakfast come up, and suddenly it was as though a curtain was pulled, displaying a new scene. The smells of water and rock and fish permeated my nose. The sun was brighter. The grass was greener.

We came to a stop near a rock, and Harrison proceeded to hide his motorcycle behind it.

"See? Not lost."

I got off the bike a little more violently than necessary, ripping the helmet off. "What was that? How did we get here?"

Harrison took the helmet from me. His short black hair was perfect after he took off his. I could only imagine what mine looked like. Frantically, I tried to finger-comb the knots out.

"It's fine. It looks fine," he said and then negated himself by moving strands this way and that.

"You didn't answer me."

"I'm not really sure. Maybe the protective magic around here was testing you. I have no idea. That magic is beyond my scope of knowledge."

"But humans can come up here?"

"Yeah, of course. There are humans in Havenwood Falls—about half the population, actually. That's the reason for the protective wards, especially the memory one."

"Memory one?"

"Memory spell, to protect our secret. If residents are away from Havenwood Falls for a complete moon cycle, we lose our memory of ever being here. Visitors lose their memory of their time here after going some miles out of the town. Twenty-five, I think. You'll forget this place when you're gone."

I flushed at his raw words.

"Harrison." I called his name, mostly to make him stop. Hearing my own cutthroat plans to leave this person, who minute by minute was burrowing into my heart, felt like a betrayal.

"What? Isn't that the truth? Or do you intend to really be mated to me and not just run after the ninety days are up and your bills are paid?"

CHAPTER 14

HARRISON

*M*y words came out harsher than I'd intended, but now was the time to be honest, while we could. Atlas looked like she couldn't care less about what I was saying. Instead, she was digging in her jeans pockets, looking for the Creator knew what.

"I'm sorry what I'm saying is so boring to you. Something I can help you find?"

All movement stopped. "Found it!"

She pulled out a hair band from her tiny pocket and swirled and twirled her hair until it was a ridiculous mess on top of her head. There was no way she was getting any helmet on her head now.

Her brown eyes squinted at me. "It wasn't boring. Stop being like that. Something you should know about me: I can't focus with my hair all over the place. It drives me insane. Give me a second to gather my thoughts on all of this."

"While you're thinking, let's go see the falls."

I reached out to take her hand, but she moved it away from me. "I can't think when you're touching me. I need to think."

My bear wanted to break free from his human chains and claim her for real right then and there. She couldn't think while I was touching her?

Damn if that didn't do it for me.

It took about ten more minutes through small climbs up rocks and turns through little caverns between hills to actually get to the waterfall. The sound of the water crashing into the pool beneath it boomed in my ears. Iridescent sprays of every blue and white in nature pummeled down and with the help of the sun, created rainbows all around us. There wouldn't be many humans around here in the November weather. The leaves, long ago turned sunset and gold, had mostly fallen to the ground and left the trees bare. The falls were even more beautiful in the winter, with the snow blanketing the rocks, turning the waterfall into stalactites of ice.

"It's stunning," Atlas said, and then grabbed the sleeve of my shirt. Still not technically touching my skin.

"There's a lot of stunning going on today."

"Stop. That's not helping the thinking."

I chuckled, harder than I had in a while. "I didn't know my mate required all this silence and not touching to think. Go on, then."

I took a few steps along the edge of the pool and crouched down to look at the tiny fish that were found nowhere else in the world. They were conjured by magic and required no food. The perfect illusions for this place.

My shoes came off next, and I rolled up the legs of my pants, sat down, and put my feet in the water like I used to when I was a kid. It was frigid, but with our higher shifter temperature, that didn't detract me from wanting to get in. Dolrich used to climb to the top and jump from the top of the falls, disturbing everything and everyone below.

I was content simply to be there.

"I did intend to mate you and leave." It was less of a statement and more of a truth blurt. As though she had to get it out of her system before there was time to think about it again.

"You did or you do?"

"What about you? Do you intend to become the next alpha or just sit around while your cousin quietly takes over? It doesn't automatically go to the heir, you know. He can choose someone else—someone who is taking diplomatic trips with him and basically being his shadow."

"How did you know? What do you know?"

Atlas's eyes rolled almost all the way to the back of her head. "I'm the only cinnamon bear to come to the castle not as a servant. You think my kin don't speak to me?"

I looked back at the water, trying to think of the few times that she'd been alone in the castle. There hadn't been very many, that I knew of.

"Who?"

She shot me a look that said *please*.

"So you can't trust me."

My skin tingled with needing her to be near for this conversation. It was probably the mating mark, but my will, when it came to my mate, was shredding by the second.

"I can trust you, Harrison. I can't trust the alpha. The more information you know, the more you can't claim ignorance to."

She shucked her shoes and mimicked my action, rolling her pants up and sitting next to me. I held my breath while she did until she threaded her fingers in my hand, still lazily laying on my thigh, desperate for her touch.

"The less I know, the less I'm responsible for."

"Yes. Do you know where the servants live? Someplace called the Terrace?"

I knew roundabout where it was, but had never been there. "I think I know where it is."

"Oscar invited me there. Wants me to see how they live. He wouldn't tell me any more than that."

The growl that ripped from my throat couldn't be stopped. Another male inviting my mate to his home wasn't something that was done, especially to the Xaviers.

My snob was showing.

"You did not just growl at me."

"No, I didn't. I actually growled at the thought of you being in another male's den."

She seemed shaken. "Oh . . . does this help?" A silky-skinned hand ran under the back of my shirt and across my back a few times. I closed my eyes, reveling in the warmth and utter comfort it gave me.

"You calmed him—us—me and my bear."

"My mom used to do that to my dad, before he died."

I nodded. Touch was a big deal to bear shifters. This was more.

"That means something, doesn't it." It wasn't a question. She knew it. Our inner animals were only calmed by our true mates.

It changed everything.

"If I'm not alpha, will you leave me?"

CHAPTER 15

ATLAS

This was the last thing I wanted. I remembered just days ago, looking at the damned blindfold and thinking that one day I would regret this.

Now I was thinking that what I once thought was a mistake might be the best thing I'd ever done.

"I had a normal life," I said, not so subtly avoiding his question.

"Tell me about your normal life."

"I had just finished nursing school. I'd been hired by the best hospital in the state. I'd secured my own apartment nearby. Plans were in place. I had plans."

I should've said plans more times. I didn't think he quite got the point.

"Had you dated? Did you have a boyfriend?"

He really had no clue about me, which was not really a surprise, seeing as how he didn't even know the state of his servants' living conditions or what they were going through on a daily basis.

"I was dating a guy. But it was nothing serious. Did you know it was Oscar who knocked on my door that night and presented the alpha right there in my new apartment filled with boxes and all my unpacked things? I didn't even have a place for him to sit. I hadn't bought furniture yet."

"It was Oscar? Why didn't he say anything the other night? Why didn't he tell me?"

"Because he's scared, Harrison. No matter how friendly and buddy-buddy he is with you, he's still just a lesser servant trying like hell to keep his job."

Out of nowhere, Harrison reached around my body and pulled me by the waist, securing me under his arm. His body was warm, almost warmer than the sun that beat down on us and the waterfall.

"I don't know how to fix all this. You were supposed to be the fix. That's what I was told. Marry you and the feud with the cinnamons was over. Done and done."

At least he called us cinnamons and not lessers. The man was learning.

"I'm just a Band-Aid to the problem, Harrison. I will appease them for a while, but it won't last, especially if . . ."

"If you don't stay."

"If I don't stay as future queen."

We were at an impasse that I never saw coming. To tell the truth, my own words had shocked me. I could only help my people by staying here and serving, and yet, my new mate, who was supposed to be the future alpha to put me in a position to actually change things, didn't want to be the alpha.

But he wanted me. The want was there in the way my heart beat around him. The way his touch made me breathless.

The way I imagined us completing the mating.

"I think we need a swim to clear our minds." Plus, I wanted to get a good look at my mate.

"You know," he used his teasing voice. I had learned to recognize it. "I didn't bring my shorts. What a shame."

"Good thing we're mated and all alone up here. What are the chances we'll get caught?"

He shrugged, looking around like he planned on getting caught right that minute. "Slim to none. There's not a lot of people who come up here. And if they do, we will scent them before they arrive."

"Okay."

"Good."

I started to get up, but Harrison had already stripped off his shirt. I hadn't seen this much of him until now. At the castle, we dressed in our separate bathrooms.

My stomach quivered with tingles from looking at him. His pecs and stomach were muscular, though I'd never seen him work out. One tiny patch of hair trailed the way to his hands, which were now unbuckling his belt.

"See something you like?" he teased again.

"Maybe. But now you have to turn around while I undress. I am so not giving you the show you gave me. No way."

"Fine." He shucked his pants and socks, and with my hand now over my eyes, I heard the splash before water droplets showered me.

"Hey!"

"Come on, Atlas. I want all of you. There's nothing to be embarrassed about."

He was right. There wasn't. Most shifters were accustomed to nudity in clans. But this was different. This was my mate and a mate I hardly knew, at that.

Drumming up all the bravery I could muster, I took off my top first and then my jeans. Bra and panties were nothing more than a glorified bikini, right?

I placed my clothes over a rock and then tiptoed through the dirt until I got to the water. It seemed like a shame to mar the beautiful scene with two skinny dippers, but that was exactly what we were about to do.

CHAPTER 16

HARRISON

I swore I thought I heard her say she was sorry to the small patch of weeds we'd sat on and flattened. She had a heart, and almost every day since I'd known her, it showed in the little things. She said thank you to the servants when we ignored them. She handed them her teacup and her plate instead of making them bow down to retrieve them.

She smiled at everyone.

She apologized to weeds.

"Did I make the fish go away?" She looked around, twirling in a circle, trying to spot the magical beings.

"I think once people are in the water, they go away. Don't worry, they'll come back."

She breathed a sigh of relief. "The water feels amazing. I thought it would be cold, but it's like the perfect warm bath."

"We can come here anytime when *you know who* isn't here."

"That's insane. You're a grown man. Wait, I don't know how old you are. How stupid is that?"

The tepid water sloshed around me as I took a few steps toward her. "Not stupid. I didn't think to ask you, either. I'm twenty-five."

"So am I."

"Birthday?"

"June thirtieth. You?"

"December fourth, but we don't really celebrate birthdays around the castle. Mom always brings a cupcake to my room at midnight. Has since I was a toddler."

Sadness, or maybe pity, drew a frown on her face. "That's awful."

"It's normal for me now."

Her hands went directly to her hips, and she made fists with them. "No, I'm not putting up with that. I want a cake, mister, and I want you to sing happy birthday to me."

Violently, I wrenched my hand through my wet hair. I couldn't let myself believe that she would actually be around a day past the ninety day probation period, much less by the time her birthday came.

One day she would go.

Another male would put his mark over mine and cause it to go away like her memories of me. She would forget our time here at the falls.

It would all fade into something she faintly remembered when she was eighty.

I didn't want to be that memory.

I wanted to make memories with her.

"I'll give you whatever kind of birthday you want."

With her gorgeous fiery brown eyes, she looked at me and smiled. Really smiled. Not the fake one she'd been giving me for the last several days, but a sincere gesture of joy.

Then her stomach rumbled. It sounded like she had the entire Kasun pack right there in her belly.

"Are you hungry, or are you carrying a triceratops in there?"

"I'm actually starving. Is there any chance we can go somewhere and get something to eat in the town? Maybe act like a normal couple for a while?"

I shrugged. "I'm not sure that normal couples skinny dip, but sure. Do you want to go home and change first?"

Her blush grew more furious. "I think we'd better. Otherwise, people in town might think . . . I don't know what they'd think."

The humans were too clueless to know any better. They wouldn't know who or what we were.

"Let's stay here a few more minutes."

My phone rang several times on the bank, but I ignored it. There were more important things to do here, like splashing my mate.

She turned to avoid the water, and I took the moment of weakness to do what I'd been craving to do for days. Damn it all if she didn't lust after me like I did.

There was nothing I wanted more than what I was about to do.

My arms encircled her waist. A gasp broke from her mouth, but she made no move to get away from me.

"This might be my favorite place now." I breathed into her ear.

She nodded. Even with the steady rhythm of the cascading water around us, her heartbeat fluttered out of control. Mine matched it beat for beat.

"I've been wanting to kiss you all day," I whispered before sucking at her tender lobe and swallowing the drop of magical water that hung there. A moan, low and slow, came from her throat. Atlas turned in the circle of my arms and wrapped hers around my neck.

"We shouldn't get attached, Harrison."

It was too late on my account. I already was. She was under my skin and pulsating through my veins.

I wanted it. All of it.

"I think I already am."

Her words said she wanted to stay away, but with every breath, her mouth came closer to mine, until I couldn't differentiate between the breaths she exhaled and the ones I inhaled.

The scent of desire filled the air around us. I was done for.

"One kiss can't hurt." She spoke to herself.

The kiss I'd intended to take from my mate began with her. She cut off my next thought by crashing her mouth down on mine. Lips that I thought would be soft surprised me by being strong and pliant at the same time. Her hands kneaded the back of my neck and pulled at the tender hairs. My only choice was to give in—give in to what she was giving me in that moment and give in to what she wanted to take from me.

I would've given her everything, surrounded by those enchanted waters with nothing between us but thin slips of material.

Frantic to get closer to her, I reached to cup the backs of her thighs and pulled her legs around my waist. As she deepened the kiss, plummeting her tongue into my mouth, her hips rocked into mine.

Atlas Xavier was everything.

Without warning, she jerked back. "That was . . ."

Fear crept into the moment. A mistake? Trouble? Fucking hot?

"It was the most incredible thing I've ever experienced," I said instead.

The coldness seeped in as she unwound her legs from my waist and lowered herself back into the water. "Weren't we supposed to go somewhere?"

My eyebrows questioned how she could hop so quickly from a moment of passion to one of ice.

"I don't trust myself here, Harrison. It's not you. You're absolutely right. That was incredible. If I stay . . . here . . . we might get lost. I would get lost."

After taking a moment to calm down and collect myself, I realized that even though we'd stopped, there was something there. A passion between us that was reeling us both in minute by minute, and there was nothing we could do to stop it. "Okay. Let's get my female some food. I know the best taco place."

Her stomach agreed with my choice.

We dressed by the waterfalls in silence. There was too much to say, yet not enough words to express it all.

We were falling into a hole that we swore wasn't there.

CHAPTER 17

ATLAS

*M*y thighs throbbed the entire way back home. I blamed it on the rumble of the motorcycle. I blamed it on the cold since leaving the water. Anything but the truth.

And the truth was, my thighs were on fire and my stomach was pulled taut because of the man in front of me. He was too attractive for his own good and certainly for mine. He was supposed to be ugly and callous and rude—all for the sake of making my break from him easy.

I shouldn't be longing for the touch of my mate.

The mate I'd never intended to keep.

When we arrived back at the castle, Harrison couldn't stop smiling. Neither could I. At least I did a little better job of hiding it. We looked like fools in love.

"Harrison!" A shrill rip of a voice called his name. At first I thought it was a wild animal, but instead, a bouncing bundle of bleached blond locks came our way and barreled into my mate.

"Sela?" What kind of name was Sela? Her arms were in a tangle around his neck, and her legs circled his waist like mine had not so long ago.

A growl, loud and pointed, bellowed from my throat, aimed right at the blond black bear.

"Sela," Harrison spoke in a dull tone. "This is my mate, Atlas."

My bear's steady disapproving rumble continued until he had successfully disengaged her from his body. Harrison came over to me, wrapped his arm around my waist, and held my hand with his other hand. As much contact as possible.

My bear relented—a little.

"Oh! Of course. I was at the mating, you know. I just came around to say hi."

This woman didn't look like someone who dropped in to give her greetings.

She looked like someone who had an agenda.

"Well, you've caught us at a bad time. My mate here was about to take me into town to get something to eat." Even I cringed at my snide tone. I wanted this female gone. I didn't like her, and she smelled like desire—around Harrison.

"Oh, fun! I'll just catch a ride with you two to do some shopping while you eat. I can find my own way back home."

Great.

"Sure. No problem. We are going to change clothes. We got a little wet at the falls."

She giggled. It was forced. "Oh, I see. Good times."

I turned to leave the area before showing her really good times.

"Hey, wait up." Harrison was behind me.

"What?"

"She's an old friend of the family. Nothing more. No more growling, female. I'm yours."

"She wants you to be hers."

"Well, I'm not. Come here." He shut the door behind him and held his arms out. I stood firm for a few seconds. I wouldn't give in that easily.

Harrison cocked his head at me.

I would give in that easily.

When my forehead met his chest and I breathed him in, my bear breathed a sigh of relief. She was content here.

"I'm sorry. I didn't mean to growl at your friend."

He laughed, and it made my head jostle around. "You didn't? It seemed pretty purposeful to me. Made me proud."

Proud.

"Why?"

"Are you serious? My mate's bear laying claim to me right there in the presence of Sela? I'm wishing we had stayed at the waterfalls to finish what we started. Then your bear would know that I am hers."

He spoke as though my bear and I weren't the same being. We were one and the same, yet as different as night and day.

He was my bear's.

And he was mine.

"Just a ride to town and then we lose her, right?" I hated to be possessive, but I had a bad feeling about little miss sunshine.

"Exactly. I promised you a date."

Without those words, I guessed he had.

"Casual?"

He chuckled, moving my hair from my face. "Jeans. A prom dress. Whatever you want. The town isn't formal and the humans might wonder why you're in your prom dress, but who cares?"

Jeans it was.

Sela sat in the back, shooting questions at Harrison that I thought were a little intrusive. Then again, five seconds after meeting her, I didn't like her.

"Dolrich said he called you a bunch of times. You didn't answer. He sent me up here to see what kind of mischief you two had gotten into."

His cousin sent his friend up to the castle to check on us? What were we, twelve?

"My lovely mate and I were exploring. Leave it at that. Dolrich needs to mind his own business."

Sela didn't appreciate that answer. In the rearview mirror, I saw her cross her arms over her chest, only to uncross them and start typing on her phone.

"Here you go, Sela. Happy shopping." Harrison had parked us on the outskirts of town. He waited until the blonde got out of the car before speaking. "That was weird, right?"

"Yeah."

He shook it off. "So, tacos or diner?"

I gave him the stink eye. "Like real tacos? Carne asada on a corn tortilla? I don't do crunchy shells and ground beef."

"Real tacos. Promise. Come on. But I should tell you something about this place before we get out of this car. Havenwood Falls is glorious and terrible, lovely and vicious, pure and murky all at the same time. We don't speak about who we are with anyone. You never know if you're speaking to a human or not. Even our bear noses can't tell the difference sometimes. The best rule is to assume human. I can't wait to show you everything."

As soon as he could, Harrison took my hand, and we walked down the streets of Havenwood Falls. He pointed out the bookstore and the coffee shop, whispering secrets to me about who owned each business and what kind of supe they were.

"Here we are."

Harrison had brought me to a Grateful Dead concert—on a food truck.

"Are we sure that's cilantro on these tacos? Or are they special tacos? I know that stuff is legal here. Are my tacos gonna make me see things?"

Not only did Harrison crack up, but so did the line of people waiting on tacos and some of the people working on the truck. I was surprised they could hear me over the lyrics of Shakedown Street.

"You're funny when you're not in the castle. Why is that?"

I shrugged. "I think that place sucks out the happiness and fun from my marrow. It's depressing. No wonder you sneak out whenever you can."

He pulled me closer. "It hasn't been so bad lately."

"Oh yeah? Why is that?" There was no hope left for me. I was a goner.

"Because I've got something to live for now."

Yep. Gone.

CHAPTER 18

HARRISON

*T*he girl could eat. The castle must have taken away her hunger, too, because she put away six tacos before I could even finish two.

"Best tacos ever, man. Righteous."

She was talking to the owner, Sky Spill Water, like she was on the road with the Dead right along with him. He'd come to sit by us after seeing my girl go after her food with such gusto. Said he was inspired by her. He was some kind of supe, but I couldn't identify what. He smelled a little like troll.

He wasn't the only one who was inspired, either. There was something about Atlas that I hadn't noticed before. Maybe it was setting her free of the castle. Maybe it was the deep-seated magic of Havenwood Falls.

Maybe it was just because Atlas was Atlas.

"This bride of yours is something else," Sky said while practically forcing a serving of flan down our throats.

"She really is," I said, waiting for her to have something in her mouth, taking away her chance to protest. Eyes cut to mine, and even around a mouthful of flan, she smiled and took my hand under the table.

I didn't know if it was the magic of the waterfall or simply getting out from under the roof of oppression, but something was happening to us. Something soul-tugging and life-altering.

I thought maybe I was falling in love with my mate.

Stupid thing to do on my part.

We bade goodbye to Sky before he tried to fill us up with more food. He invited us to some kind of outdoor concert, but Atlas spoke up quickly and made our excuses.

"I couldn't eat another thing. That place was so good."

"I've actually never eaten there."

She cracked up. "Oh, Harrison, you're such a snob. "

Well, that hurt. She wasn't wrong, on the same coin.

"I am. Wanna help me with that?"

"Help you with not being snobby? Sure. Pick up that penny."

I looked down at the sidewalk where she pointed. Pennies were dirty and not even worth their weight in copper.

"Why?" That was my first question.

"Just do it."

"It's . . ." I hadn't realized I had such an aversion to coins.

"Pick up the damned penny. I'll give you a reward later if you do."

The penny was in my hand before she could finish her sentence.

"For the rest of the day, you have to wave to people in town and smile."

"That sounds painful."

Reaching between us, she took my hand in hers. "Trust me, the rewards will be good."

"Hello!" I yelled to the first person I saw and waved like a lunatic.

Ronya Augustine, one of the mages, didn't wave back. Her lip curled at my out-of-character greeting, and as we passed her, she mumbled something under her breath that even my shifter hearing couldn't make out.

Soon she'd forgotten our deal, enamored by the town square. "Oh! Look how beautiful. It reminds me of the Gilmore Girls!"

I didn't know who the Gilmore Girls were or why the town square reminded her of them, but whoever they were had her eyes lit up like the lights for the fallen at the Festival of Lights in January.

I'd snuck into the Festival of Lights one time with Dolrich. He ended up tattling on us. We were fifteen.

"Who are the Gilmore Girls?" I asked.

She looked at me, incredulous. "Are you serious right now? If we weren't already mated, that would be a deal breaker."

"I'm totally serious."

"It's a show. This epic-cult-like show. Never mind. The binge starts tonight."

I nodded. For the next hour, we stayed around town square. She made us take selfies in the gazebo, and I swore she touched every pumpkin, cornucopia, and turkey in the square.

Ridiculous.

And adorable.

"So where's the Terrace?"

This again.

I was hoping she would forget that part. My father warned me to never go to the Terrace. It was where the lesser servants lived. It was not for royalty.

It was strange that one instant, my father shielded me from the things that only royalty should know, but in the same breath be offended that I wasn't alpha material.

"I think it's this way."

We went down Main Street right off town square, and I looked up at a few apartments on the second floor over the retail shops at ground level. Most of the businesses around town square had offices or apartments above them. The Terrace was a group of apartments above the butcher shop.

"I think that's it."

Atlas took my hand. "Come on."

We went up the stairs off the back alley and knocked on the dilapidated door. Someone had poured salt across the threshold, outside the door. They must've been expecting evil to try to cross.

"Who is it?" A familiar voice called from the other side.

"It's Atlas and Harrison," Atlas called through the door.

After a few turns of locks and what sounded like a chain, the door opened, but just a sliver.

"Come in. Most of the staff are at the castle, but the rest of us are off since the alpha is away."

Oscar gave Atlas a look. He was scared. Why was my childhood friend scared of me?

"It's okay," Atlas said. "He knows how to keep his mouth shut. So this is it? For how many people?"

The place was like a refugee camp. Each area was the size of a dorm room, and that was being generous. Atlas covered her mouth and nose, but not before I saw her mouth gaping open at the horrific sights of squalor. Cots were stacked right next to each other, and most were on their last leg. Some were so broken that their owners had laid them to rest on the bare floor. There was no place for a couch, and the kitchen consisted of a two-burner stove and a sink smaller than those in our guest bathrooms. The windows were covered in newspapers duct-taped to the panes. The paint peeled from the walls, and the floors were stripped, concrete-cold, and naked. Smells of sweat and tears made my eyes burn with the stench. This was no place for any creature.

This place was paid for by my father. Why was he having them live like this? They may be servants, but they were bears just like us.

"You live here, Oscar?" My heartbeat thumped heavily in my chest as I waited for him to answer. I almost felt betrayed by my friend. If he was living like this, I could've done something. I would've spoken to my father.

"This is where the men sleep. The women servants and your father's women are in the next apartment over."

"But you're married, Oscar. You have a mate."

He hung his head, as though I'd reminded him of his worst nightmare.

"We are not allowed to sleep in the same room with our mates."

My hands went to my hips. I looked left and right wondering what in the fuck was going on.

"Why not?"

Oscar's head hung again. Atlas chimed in. "Oscar, give us a few minutes, okay? We'd like to see the female quarters next."

He nodded and went to the sink, ran the water, and started to wash a motley crew of mismatched dishes.

"Harrison, listen to me." With her hand fisting the front of my shirt, Atlas pulled me closer. She wasn't angry. I could feel the desperation coming off her in waves of scent through our ever-strengthening bond. "Your father did this. Don't you understand? This is only one of the many things he keeps from you. He doesn't want his servants sleeping together, because what happens when married couples sleep together?"

My eyes had been focused on her mouth while she spoke, but with her question, they raised to her eyes. "They have cubs."

"Yes, and if you loathe an entire population, what's the last thing you want them to do?"

My shoulders slumped, and the room began to spin. "Procreate."

"Exactly. Your father is essentially keeping his servants sterile. There is someone from the castle who comes every night and locks the apartments from the outside to make sure the mates can't get to each other. Your father is a special kind of dictator, right under your nose. It's no wonder he doesn't want you going with him to meetings. He loves to keep you ignorant."

She let go of my shirt, and I wavered on my feet. With my hand on the wall, I braced myself for whatever was to come next.

"Oscar, can you show us the rest? Please? We are so sorry to interrupt your day off." I ground out the polite words.

"It's okay. My mate is working anyway. We have opposite days off."

We took a five-minute tour of the rest of the place. The female quarters were as sparse as the rest. Five hundred thousand thoughts pummeled through my mind, along with limitless questions.

"You said something about my father's women? What does that mean?"

Atlas took my hand, trying to console me. "Come on, Harrison. We can talk about this later."

"No." I pushed Atlas's hand away. "Tell me now. This shit is enough. I'm not some helpless spoiled prince. Tell me the fucking truth. I've obviously been lied to all my life. Oscar, please, if you ever considered me a friend, tell me the truth."

A light blazed in Oscar's eyes, and before Atlas could speak, he stepped forward. "You know what? I'll tell you, Harrison. I don't even care if you punish me or banish me or whatever. It's time. Your father keeps a harem of sorts here. He calls on them night and day. Sometimes they get pregnant, and he makes sure they get taken care of when they do. We make minimum wage working for your father while we serve him steak on a golden platter. He hides everything from you. Everything."

"Why hasn't the Court stopped this? Why haven't they stepped in? It's their duty to protect the supes who live here."

Oscar bowed up against me. "Because your father makes deals with demons. He has one named Justus Abbadon that he deals with to keep this place under some kind of glamour. We don't know what the deal is exactly and to tell you the truth, we don't want to know. We have reported it to the Court, but what they see is nothing but façade. They see a five-star hotel when they look in here, and then think we are nuts for reporting it. I think Ric suspects something is going on here. He stops in from time to time, but with the demon working for your father, despite his sense that something is off, Ric can't make a case. Your father has so many ill-willed supes in his pocket, I'm surprised he can keep track. One of the mages must be involved, too, covering up the demon's magic."

This must be why my father hated the Kasuns and the rest of the Court so much. They suspected that he was up to something.

I thought back on my life for some clues. For some reason, my mind scrambled for an argument against Oscar's accusations. That was easier than accepting what he was saying. This was my father. Why would he betray the son who would one day take over his job?

Maybe because I was never intended to be alpha.

"What about the news? There are servants who read the news to him. I get copies of it by email. Why haven't I heard about this?"

Atlas reached for my hand, but I moved out of the way again. There was nothing anyone could do to soothe me now.

"Harrison, your father doesn't let any news enter the castle that doesn't involve absolutely bowing down to him. And Oscar says he's heard of a plan to get rid of me as soon as you become alpha—if you become alpha."

My pulse drummed between my temples, and the pain almost blinded me. "I can't hear any more."

I walked out, around cots and blankets full of holes, to the outside, where I was finally able to catch a breath of fresh air.

This wasn't happening.

"I'm going home," I announced and started down the stairs.

"Harrison?" Atlas came to the door. Her voice was tiny, and desperation hung from the tip of it. "You're leaving me here?"

Of course I wasn't.

I turned, only about ten steps down, and faced her. I was ashamed and could barely bring myself to look her in the eye. I was part of this. I was under this regime that branded and burned her people.

I was at the root of her pain—the pain of her kin.

And I was too ignorant to even know it.

"Of course not. I'm sorry. Come with me. Atlas, stay with me."

The look on my mate's face broke me. She was in me and with me and swirling through me and burrowed so deep, I wouldn't ever be able to get her out.

I didn't ever want to. And I'd be damned if my father ever touched her.

She didn't move, so I pushed further. "Atlas, let's go home, love."

She turned to say goodbye to Oscar and gave him some empty promises about trying to make it better.

Oscar didn't come out to say goodbye.

I didn't blame him.

"Hey, I don't want to go home yet. Is there a place we can get a cup of coffee or something?"

A cup of coffee would wake me up, and at this point, I wanted a drink that took the edge off the rage that was brewing in my chest.

"I've got a better idea."

Taking her hand, I led us to The Dirty Knuckle. The bar was frequented by humans and supes alike. I'd only been once.

"Oh, nice. Coffee was just for conversation. I see you're looking for a reprieve."

I turned on her, swift and steady. "I'm looking for a fucking way out of this life that is blowing up all around me. The only thing in it that's worth anything to me is you. You understand? The one person I thought would be fleeting is now the only one who is solid."

CHAPTER 19

ATLAS

*S*howing Harrison what I'd seen in the past three days—what he hadn't known in his twenty-five years being here—wasn't easy.

But it had to be done.

"I'm here. I'm not going anywhere." I spoke the words that were truth now. Harrison and I were too deeply bound to be separated now.

He had to know that this seemingly perfect life he had grown up seeing wasn't real. It was all an elaborate scheme to keep a race of bears under the alpha's thumb and powerless to stop him.

We were served our drinks by a lithe and lanky fae who introduced himself as Casten. I'd heard there were some Seelie in the world, but had never seen one in person. He smelled like cotton candy and the sweetest caramel apple to me.

Harrison said nothing to me during the hour we were in the bar. Despite his fervor to drink his cares away, my mate mostly kept his face buried in his hands, never touching the drink that was placed on the table in front of us.

"When did you know?" he asked when we got back in the car.

"Oscar approached me the day after our mating. There was no time to waste, Harrison. Do you even know where your father is?"

"He's at a meeting. He took Dolrich."

I slapped my hand over my face. He was so blind, it bordered on ridiculous. But under the regime of his father, there was no way for him to know better. That's what I was there for. My purpose was clear. If nothing else, Harrison Xavier would wake up and know the truth of the masquerade his father conducted.

"Harrison, your father is in Nebraska, securing a containment camp of sorts." I choked over the word containment. They gave a cage such a pretty name.

"A containment camp? And my mother knows? And Dolrich?"

"I don't know for sure, but I'm assuming."

He turned to me, now doing eighty miles an hour on the road to the castle. "Oh? What do you mean? What, four days here and you don't know every facet of the royal plans?"

I forgave him that one. He was in pain and angry. It was written all over his face, and we were smothering in the scent of it, trapped in this car.

"They are going to put all of the cinnamon bears in one place so your father can control the numbers. That's the nice version. The not-so-nice version is that he's going to cage bears like me." I took his hand off the seat belt, to which he was hanging on for dear life, and put it against my chest. I wanted him to feel the truth inside me. My need was desperate and didn't make any sense. "They are going to cage us and then starve us to death, Harrison. Do you want that for me? For my mother? For my best friend Sammy?"

Seconds later, we were at a full stop on the side of the road. "How can you say that? I want you with me. I know we started this as an arranged mating, but there's more here. And I'll be damned if I let your people suffer. I won't."

I shrugged. I needed this flame inside him to grow. He needed to be fueled to full in order to fight his father.

And I needed his strength to build my own.

I needed my mate to fight this tyranny with me.

"But what are you going to do? You don't want to be alpha. You've pretty much set it up where Dolrich is going to be alpha. You think he'll be any different? You think they're gonna let us stay together while he plans for my people's demise? Please. I'll be in the cage with the rest of them. And by the way, you know your friend Sela?"

He nodded. I suspected he was afraid to interrupt. I would be afraid to interrupt me right in that moment.

"She's in bed with Dolrich. She's your new alpha queen, and you don't even know it."

His eyebrows bunched in the middle above his nose. "Is that why you growled at her?"

I blushed against my will. "I don't know."

"No." Harrison took my face in his almost burning hands and gently made me face him. "You can't start being shy now, Atlas. We are thick in this together. You understand? I think I've made it clear how I feel about you. Now you tell me why you growled at Sela."

Ugh. Sela.

"Because she was on you like a wolf on a sheep. And it pissed me off, and possibly she just had more physical contact with you in that moment than I have in a week, and it was killing me."

With a flick of his wrist, he unbuckled the seatbelt, and his mouth was on mine. Lips that started out as greedy and bordering on violent quickly turned gentle yet passionate. His hands were now on my hips, tugging at them, needing a closeness that the confines of this car just wouldn't give us. Anger laced his movements, and I took each lashing from him, knowing that his heart was now changed.

"I'm taking us home," he said, breathless, breaking the kiss for just those four words.

"Fast as you can."

My head was still spinning with thoughts of what had just happened while he buckled back up and sped to the castle. Servants were in the living quarters, so we had to act normal as Harrison took my hand and led me to the bedroom. Once there, his lips were on mine, leaving them only for the few seconds it took to relieve ourselves of shirts and jeans and shoes.

"This is real, Atlas. Tell me this is real. Everything in my life is a fucking lie except you. Tell me this is real."

I couldn't form the words yet, but he needed to know. He needed to realize that this was the beginning of everything that was real for him and for us.

I kissed the mark I'd made on his shoulder as he kneaded my back and skimmed his hands down my sides, gently brushing the sides of my breasts.

"Harrison, you and I are real. I tried to deny you, but I can't. I won't anymore. Touch me and know that this mating is real. You are mine." The word mine was backed by my bear, turning the word into a growl.

"Mine. You are mine and no one else's, and you will be my queen." His bear mimicked mine, enforcing those words with his own voice. "You are absolutely stunning, Atlas." With a finger under my chin, he commanded that I look at him, seeing the raw truth in his almost-black eyes. His other hand pulled down a strap of my copper-colored lace bralette. "We have to say the words, mate, or I can't go any further. Tell me."

I whimpered at the thought of him stopping.

"Look at me, Atlas, and say the words."

Barely able to harness my want enough to speak, I looked into the soft caring eyes of my mate and recited the words I knew. "I take you, Harrison Xavier, as my mate and my other half until my body fails me and death takes me."

He repeated the words to me, all while doing things with his hands that rendered me putty in his care.

He and I became one.

CHAPTER 20

HARRISON

a knock on the door pulled me from a deep sleep I didn't know I was capable of. I looked down to see Atlas, now my mate in every way, draped across my chest, her chestnut hair sparkling, reflecting the little bit of dawn that was streaming through the curtains.

"What?"

I didn't even bother getting up or covering the bits that were hanging out. They could just shut their eyes. I did, however, cover up Atlas.

"Harrison, I mean, sir, something has happened." It wasn't my usual servant. In fact, this was one dressed in black, which meant that he worked on my father's side of the castle.

"What happened that warranted waking my mate up?" Atlas now turned in the bed next to me.

"It's your father, sir. There was an accident with the plane. He was coming home early. The alpha is dead, sir."

I jumped from the bed, grabbing the robe that I never used but was always there.

"And my mother?"

He bowed his head, and for a microsecond, I thought she was gone as well. "Your mother is well, sir. The—I shouldn't say."

My voice rose. "Damn it. I don't care what you think you should and shouldn't say. Tell me now!"

"Your mother asked Ms. Beaumont to put a safety spell on her before they left. Your father refused the magic. The alpha queen is on her way back to the castle."

I wanted to shift into my animal right that second and chase down my mother en route to make sure she arrived safely.

All I could think about was my mother and her safety. Every thought was trained on her.

For my father, I was numb. For all the things I now knew about him. For all the things I knew about him since birth. In all the ways he'd betrayed our people and his own son.

The only tears I would shed would be for the father I'd never had.

"What is your name?" I pointed the question to the servant, who was now shaking.

"Tobias," he answered.

"Tobias, from this moment forward, until I tell you not to, you need to give me updated information about my mother's safety. Have I made myself clear?"

"Yes, Alpha." The servant ticked his head to the left, baring his neck to me in submission and then left.

Alpha. He called me Alpha.

"Atlas," I whispered, climbing back into the bed. Her eyes were open, but she hadn't moved. "Did you hear that? My father is gone."

"You are alpha. And I'm the . . . and your mother. Your cousin." With incomplete sentences, she'd said so much. My body was icy and solid like it was made from frozen metal. Other than the worry over my mother, my mind was blank, and the absence of sympathy shook me.

"I am the alpha now. There is no other choice. I won't accept any other fate. We have to go see to my mother. Let's get dressed."

Atlas pulled the sheet off of her body and rolled out of bed. We were both exhausted from the night before, but there was no time for sleep.

"I'm sorry. This isn't quite the morning I'd imagined." I pulled her to me after opening the robe to welcome her into my warmth.

"Fate doesn't care what you imagined, Harrison. It simply knows what it wants out of you."

CHAPTER 21

ATLAS

*W*e dressed and went down to the main hall to wait for Divine to arrive home safely. From the gossip of the servants, who were now not too scared to speak to us, we heard that Emilian died on impact when the plane crashed. Divine, kept safe by an enchantment that was done at the same time as my tattoo, was without a scratch. She was safe but very much shaken.

"Alpha, she's here. Coming up the drive, and so is Dolrich," Tobias whispered to us. Regardless of the circumstances, the death of the alpha was felt in the servants' hearts. Their faces and tears said it all.

"Thank you." Harrison had scarcely let go of me during the entire morning. When I wasn't under the protection of his arm, we were tethered by our hands. He said nothing in regard to his father, but I felt the unrest in his heart over the issue. There was fear in his scent—a slip of unknowing in his voice when he spoke to me.

Divine came in, tired and in mourning for her husband, but physically fine. We stayed in her room for the day and most of the night, simply to be there in case she needed anything or just someone to talk to. Harrison had intercepted most of the alpha's advisors, who were already attempting to pressure Divine into choosing this kind of service or that kind of coffin.

"He won't be buried," Divine said in a faraway voice in the middle of the night.

"Mother, tell me what you would have me do, and I will do it." My mate was desperate to make Divine as comfortable as possible.

"He wanted to be cremated—scattered to the wind on the peaks of the mountains behind the castle. Not be buried beside his mate. No place for me to visit in his absence."

"If that's what you want, that's what we will do." Harrison took her hand.

With no warning, Divine got up from her bed and faced us. She grabbed my hand in one of hers and Harrison's in the other. "Promise me that you will do better. Unite our kingdom and bring together our people. There was nothing I could do to help under your father, but you two have a new start. Bring about change. Love each other. And never allow this castle to come between the bond that seals you. This bond will make sure you succeed. Promise me."

Harrison promised. Shortly afterward, she requested time alone, and we granted her request without hesitation.

We walked out of Divine's room hand in hand. As the doors closed behind us, a gathering of the castle's servants and staff stood before us.

"Alpha. Queen." Each bowed after baring their necks to my mate, the new alpha, and me, the cinnamon bear that was now their queen.

"Not quite." Dolrich spoke above the rest.

CHAPTER 22

HARRISON

"*D*olrich, I see you made it out unharmed." Then my cousin, whom I'd known all my life, changed before me, not into a bear, but into something far more sinister. He unbuttoned his suit jacket, and the expression on his face morphed into that of a stranger.

"You think that was by accident? Please. You've always been a bit of a dunce, even when we were kids. But I'm not."

Atlas lunged a little at the man that dared to insult me in my own home, but I stepped in front of her. If Dolrich caught hell from anyone, it was going to be me.

Stepping forward, I pulled all the bravery I could into my voice. "Dolrich, I know you and my father were involved in some kind of arrangement, but with his death, the position of alpha falls to me, his son. Unless you have something in writing with his alpha seal, there is nothing that would name you alpha."

A grin, menacing and vile, took shape while he laughed. "That is, unless there is a challenge."

Gasps broke out from the crowd around us. I didn't want a challenge with Dolrich. No matter what, he was my family, and a challenge would mean that one of us would never leave the battlefield.

"There will be no challenge. How did you survive this tragedy with my mother while my father died?"

He laughed, and the booming sound reverberated against the marble floors and walls of my father's wing of the castle.

"See?" He addressed the servants. "He is the stupidest son of an alpha there ever was. I've taken over his father's favor, taken over this kingdom, and then killed his father. Yet he stands there like a fool asking why and how? I killed him! The same spell that protects this palace was put on me, while your mother was protected by one of those people on the Court." He spat the word *Court*, sounding like the twin of my late father. "The cinnamon bears were going to kill him anyway. They were the pilots flying the plane. I simply joined in on the fun."

"What?" Atlas stepped forward, her words holding a desperation I recognized well.

"Oh yes, the princess thought she had stepped in and gotten her neck bitten and just like that," he snapped his fingers, "every bit of hate harbored by those lesser bears would be solved. You were wrong, little cinnamon bear. Your kind were quietly waiting in the wings to kill him anyway, marriage or not. Your kind have always been lesser in this kingdom and always will be. But don't worry, when I send all the lessers to the encampment, I won't separate you from your dear mate. You two make an incredibly vapid pair."

Enough was enough. This man was no family of mine, just like my dead father was no family of mine. He wouldn't stand there and admit to helping murder the alpha and imprisoning an entire race of bears without consequences. I was born to be the alpha of this kingdom of black bears and cinnamon bears alike—to realign our races as one species united.

Even if it meant killing Dolrich.

"Are you with me?" I turned to Atlas.

Her eyes bored into mine as she tried to figure out my plan.

"I'm with you."

"Dolrich, I challenge you for the position of alpha. I won't stand for any upheaval in the ranks, including yours. Whoever is still standing after the challenge becomes alpha. That way, when my people look to me, they will know I hold the position without opposition."

"What?" Atlas whimpered.

"It has to be done. We will never rest with him alive, and this kingdom will never be at peace until we have an alpha who is ready to take some action."

"This should be fun," Dolrich answered, with a confidence that I despised.

"I'm with you," my mate, now holding my hand, repeated.

CHAPTER 23

ATLAS

I expected the challenge to take place in a week or so. Instead, my mate announced that the challenge would take place only two hours later. Two fucking hours later.

He dragged me to our wing of the castle to await the fight. Dolrich would wait his turn outside the castle. Served him right. Even as a cousin, he didn't deserve to stay in our home a second longer. As the door shut behind us, palpable fear settled in the pit of my stomach. The fear I'd barely contained on the night of our mating was child's play next to this terror. Harrison sat on the window seat where we had marked each other.

"You can't do this, Harrison. All you have to do is have Dolrich tried by the Bear High Council in Alaska for murder or accessory to murder. He won't become alpha that way. Your mother is in her room grieving. Don't make her grieve a son and a husband on the same day. Don't make me a widow."

Before I muttered another word, Harrison's hands were on my shoulders, and the focused, stern look on his face frightened me. "I am the alpha. I won't lose. I've been losing all my life. Hiding in this castle. Taking whatever was given to me without question. My life and yours and the future of our kingdom rides on this fight. I won't lose. You hear me?"

His eyes grew darker as he spoke to me, bearing down on my own. Hearing the hard decision in his voice, I knew there was nothing I could do. Finally, this mate of mine who had stood in the shadows all of his life, some of his own making and some put over him, was now becoming what he was born to be.

It was about fucking time.

Despite the fight, watching this evolution was only making me fall in love further.

I put my hands on either side of his face and leaned in so that our noses touched. "I believe in you, Harrison. You are the true alpha of this kingdom, and alphas don't lose a fight."

"That's my girl." The pride came off him in waves, along with a tinge of fear and trepidation. Fear was inevitable. It would strengthen him in battle.

We stared into each other's eyes for what seemed like hours, though I knew it was only minutes. "Harrison, let's not waste this time."

The last word barely escaped my mouth before his lips crashed down on mine with a force that bordered on dangerous. His words conveyed bravery, but his kiss said this may be our last.

Our clothes were scattered around the room in a matter of seconds, and all else was forgotten, or at least, shoved to the backs of our minds. The air around us crackled with a new power. Our bond now emitted the power of an alpha couple. His inner strength entangled with mine as we deepened our bond in that span of time between our past and our future.

Afterward, we lay together in silence, constantly touching and reaffirming all the things we had yet to say.

Chest to chest, we contented ourselves with simply being close.

"It's time for me to go," Harrison groaned before placing a kiss on the tip of my nose.

"I know."

He moved to get out of the bed, but I stopped him with my hand gripping his arm. "You fight like hell, Harrison. You kill that bastard for trying to take away what is yours by right. He'll kill me if he becomes alpha, and if he gets the chance, your mother too. Don't let him take away my family."

That was the first time I'd called my new mate my family.

"He won't take anything away from me." I let him leave, but instead of walking away to get dressed, he turned to me. "You know I love you, right? I know you meant to leave me just like I meant to let you go, but fate had other plans. I'm fucking in love with you, Atlas Xavier."

"I fucking love you too, Harrison Xavier, alpha of the Black Bears."

We both laughed before we dressed, stealing glances at each other with each stitch of clothing.

DOLRICH AND HARRISON met on the front lawn in front of the castle and then proceeded to the fields in the back, beyond the gardens. This would be a battle to the death. Challenges for the position of alpha came with no rules. There would only be one victor. One hole would be dug for the defeated.

I barely contained my shiver as I watched Oscar begin the battle with some kind of muttered words, said too softly for even my shifter ears to hear.

Harrison gave me one look and a wink before I heard the first shattering of bones. They both shifted into their animal counterparts at once. It was the fastest shift I'd ever seen in my life. Most of our kind took their time in shifting, to manage the pain and allow their bears to take over their consciousness.

With the anger like a thick blanket over us all, their shift was fueled in a matter of seconds.

Harrison's bear took a minute to find his comfort zone. His sheer size made my chest constrict. Other than a few males in my old clan, I'd never seen a black bear reach almost seven feet in height when shifted. One of his rounded ears, tipped with cinnamon, twitched, ready for action. A roar boomed through the open space, filling my ears and causing me to shiver. He swayed from foot to foot, getting used to the shift.

And while he did, Dolrich made his first strike, right at Harrison's belly.

I gasped and slapped my hand over my mouth to quell the scream. I was beat by another hand, a hand that smelled familiar. "Don't scream, my dear. He will become distracted by your fear. If you can, propel all your bravery and love to him. Your connection is strong. My son will be able to hear you—to feel your strength build on his." Divine spoke to me with her face close to my ear and her other arm wrapped around my body. That arm was the only thing keeping me upright as Dolrich continued to blast Harrison with blow after blow.

Closing my eyes, I pictured my energy, all the power and courage I could muster, being a strong gust of wind that flowed to Harrison in the air with the force of a winter storm.

"There you go, dear. It's working. See your mate. He is strong because of you."

Divine held me tighter around my waist, murmuring comforting words as Harrison began to fight back. He slashed at Dolrich's chest and abdomen, making contact time after time.

The pair went at each other like bears in the wild over a female, except this was no mating war. This was war for a kingdom.

I thought Harrison was winning, and he was, until Dolrich bent and tore three shreds into Harrison's thigh, causing him to falter and crash to the ground at Dolrich's feet. Dolrich took advantage of the position and punched Harrison on his skull with a force that I swore shook the ground below us.

"He needs to hear you now, Atlas. Scream his name. Make him remember why he fights. Yes, he wants to be alpha, but the needs of his mate will come before it all."

I opened my mouth, but nothing came out. The shaking had taken over my body. Behind me, Divine sweetly cheered me on until sweetness, she realized, wasn't quite working. "Now, Atlas. Don't you let my son die!"

Her scream somehow became my own as I used my every

capability to cry to my mate, to let him know that I loved him, to know that he could not lose, to let him know that he wasn't alone.

"There. Look. His eyes have opened. He sees you."

Across the field, Harrison was alert and had lunged forward, taking a gaping bite out of Dolrich's leg. With his cousin now seriously wounded and bleeding, my mate, the alpha, went in for the kill. His movements were pointed and stealthy again. His blows, each and every one, were sharp and targeted at his prey.

And with one final swipe of Harrison's bear claws at Dolrich's throat, it all was over.

Harrison took one look at me before passing out and shifting back to human.

Before I could reach him, he was taken into the castle. Oscar and Thad cleaned his wounds and had him resting in the bed while I watched on, silently praying and not so silently weeping.

"He is going to be fine. His wounds will heal soon. He is a strong shifter. We have a powerful alpha. Is there anything else you need, Alpha Queen?"

The only thing I needed was for Harrison to wake up.

EPILOGUE

HARRISON

*en months later*

EVEN WITH THE drive that Atlas and I had for changing the kingdom, the evolution of people's thinking came slowly.

We had completed some immediate tasks that couldn't be left for later.

The Terrace was renovated and given to Oscar and his mate as one apartment for the couple. The rest of the servants were moved to other housing in Havenwood Falls until we could find a more permanent solution.

My father's harem was dissolved and relocated to Texas, per my queen's request.

The land in Nebraska, bought for the sole purpose of containing the cinnamon bears, was sold back to the grizzlies.

But not everyone was pleased about what we were doing. The more conservative black bears didn't take well to the integration of cinnamon bears into the fold.

They were less than joyful when Atlas and I announced that she was pregnant with not one, but three bears that I hoped looked like her and possessed her fire to help others.

"I can't breathe," Atlas huffed, coming into my office. I'd been in there all day for most of the ten months, trying to figure out how to reform my father's stupid ways of running the kingdom.

I jumped from the chair. "Let's go to the hospital."

Her eyebrows bunched. She looked at me as though I was growing another head. "Going to the hospital isn't going to change the fact that I have three cubs that think my lungs are a trampoline. They still need time to cook."

"Come here, mate. Let me see if I can talk some sense into them."

I scooted back and made room for her on my lap. The female who had once intended to leave me as soon as she could now had quite the stock in our people and our kingdom. She worked almost as much as I did, even with three cubs inside her.

"Right here."

She giggled. "Really? All four of us on your lap?"

"Yes. I'm pretty damned strong."

"Fine, but don't say I didn't warn you."

She sat on my knees, and I tucked her into my body the best I could.

"Okay, little ones, this is your alpha speaking." I rubbed along her belly, bare now that she'd pulled up her shirt. "You have to let your mother rest and breathe. Be good in there. Not much longer until you're born."

I looked up at Atlas to see if she was laughing at me or loving it. Except my mate, this strong and tough female who'd opened the doors of life and truth for me, was fast asleep, her head against my shoulder. Her eyes fluttered in her sleep, probably dreaming of all the things we had to conquer together when she woke.

Sometimes, I imagined where I would be without her. Probably still a pampered and ignorant prince, safe and witless in this brick prison.

"I love you," she murmured, either to the babes or me.

"I love you, Alpha Queen."

~

WE HOPE you enjoyed this story in the Havenwood Falls series of novellas featuring a variety of supernatural creatures. Keep going for an excerpt of *Ink & Fire* by R.K. Ryals. The series is a collaborative effort by multiple authors.

Other books you may enjoy in the main Havenwood Falls series:

Old Wounds by Susan Burdorf
Fate, Love & Loyalty by E.J. Fechenda
Flames Among the Frost by Amy Hale
Defying Gravity by Kallie Ross

Also look for the YA line, Havenwood Falls High; the historical paranormal line, Legends of Havenwood Falls; the darker, sexier side of town, Havenwood Falls Sin & Silk; and the local supernatural college, Sun & Moon Academy.

Immerse yourself in the world of Havenwood Falls and stay up to date on news and announcements at www.HavenwoodFalls.com.

ABOUT THE AUTHOR

Lila Felix is full of antics and stories. She refused to go to kindergarten after the teacher made her take a nap on the first day of school. She staged her first protest in middle school. She almost flunked out of her first semester at Pepperdine University because she was enthralled with their library and frequently was locked in. Now her husband and three children have to put up with her rebel nature in Louisiana, where her days are filled with cypress trees, crawfish, and of course her books and writing. She writes about the ordinary people who fall extraordinarily in wild, true love.

ACKNOWLEDGMENTS

I can't thank my husband and kids enough for always having my back.

And Jaime, who does all the things for me.

Thanks to Kristie Cook, for having a vision that spans time and space and brilliance and glory. If Havenwood Falls were real, she would be the queen of them all.

For allowing me to borrow Casten (Seelie) and Justus (demon), I have to thank Heather Hildenbrand and AnnaLisa Grant. I can't wait until these guys have debuts of their own.

To the authors of all the Havenwood Falls novels: You make the writing world not so lonely.

~ A Havenwood Falls New Adult Novella ~

HAVENWOOD FALLS

INK & FIRE

R.K. RYALS

Ink & Fire (A Havenwood Falls Novella) by R.K. Ryals

It takes the fallen to save the damned.

Harper Sinclair doesn't own any books. If she can avoid it, she doesn't read or write at all. Words are dangerous. Beyond the cover of a book, words rearrange themselves for Harper, becoming messages from beyond. Brutal messages. Terrible messages. When she writes, awful things flow from her fingers. She's a spiritual writer haunted by demons.

Lucas Fox is one of the fallen, an angel whose murderous past keeps him from Heaven. Whose protective, chivalric nature keeps him from Hell. He lives between worlds, content to enjoy his vices while doing just enough to keep him out of the underworld.

But when Harper is forced to sign a contract for a house she buys in Havenwood Falls, the words that appear aren't her name. Instead, she pens a dire message threatening a fallen angel whose old alliance with a ruler of Hell has made him a target of a powerful demon lord. A warning that draws Lucas Fox to Havenwood Falls to settle old scores and puts Harper Sinclair directly in the line of danger.

INK & FIRE

AN EXCERPT

Prologue

Danger rises in the darkness. Shadows weave in and out of nothingness, the Infernum a screaming mess of imagined pain, for the fear of pain is often much worse than the actual hurt.

Distorted, faceless creatures march through an empty space filled with evil intentions. Trapped, they beg for mercy.

In the midst of chaos, a man's face appears, as beguiling as it is dreadful. Hair the color of midnight, dark eyes touched with crimson, and a hard face lined with smoke and madness stares into emptiness.

The Infernum swallows its prisoners whole.

But not for long. Not for one of them.

"The time has come." Lips curl in a sickening smile, a forked tongue darting out to taste the air.

Chapter 1

My aunt once told me that anything I ever needed to know about life I could find in a Van Morrison song. Apparently, she'd experienced all of her firsts to his music: first date, first kiss, and her first time losing her virginity. I say first because my aunt is continually losing her virginity. Something about taking it back and starting over every time she feels let down by an experience. At forty-eight years old and after a recent less-than-satisfying encounter, Eloise Sinclair is now a virgin again.

Hanging turquoise beads *click click* together as Eloise exits the back of her new age shop Into the Mystic, cradling a steaming mug, the contents smelling suspiciously of mugwort and bourbon. The mugwort is for enhancing her psychic abilities. The bourbon is for her nerves.

A long-sleeved purple tunic swings against polka-dotted leggings as she approaches me, wisps of auburn hair falling into perceptive brown eyes. "The Pen Is Mightier Than the Sword."

She raises her mug at me. The Van Morrison song title is all it takes. I've heard way too much of my aunt's music playlist. She's relating my life to the song.

"Do your clients enjoy translating Morrisonese, or is this just for my benefit?" I grimace at the song choice. "Wrong one for me."

"You assume."

"If this is about the meeting I have at the plaza this afternoon—"

"It's about your fate," Eloise cuts me off cryptically.

My family makes deals with destiny, usually other people's. It pays the rent and the utility bills. The mugwort and the bourbon, too. For prices ranging anywhere from one hundred to three hundred dollars an hour—all depending on the type of reading—my aunt Eloise can discern a client's future, past, or present.

She is psychic. I am, too. Only, my abilities come with a curse. A rather inconvenient one.

Eloise studies me over the rim of her mug, her gaze raking over my loose brown hair and makeup-less green eyes before dropping to my solid navy sweatshirt and skinny jeans. "You couldn't have tried a little harder for such a momentous occasion?"

I glance down at myself. "For picking up a set of keys?"

"Hmm."

My gaze roams over the shop, careful not to linger on anything too long. This shop and the basement apartment downstairs are home. For the last twenty-three years, it has been everything. The purple walls, the brightly painted bookshelves stocked with new age books, the scarf-covered tables littered with candles, the glass cases full of jewelry and crystals, the mauve and gold chaise lounge, the stuffed blue-checked chairs, the herbal tea counter, and the beaded curtains leading to the basement stairs and the back of the shop all wail at me. Memories have a way of making inanimate objects speak.

Or maybe I am just super emotional.

"Did you 'hmm' at me?" I ask, following Aunt Eloise to the front door.

She flips over the open sign, arches a brow, and hmms again.

Outside, the morning sun sweeps like spilled pastel paints down Eleventh Street, the rays turning the light dusting of snow on the shop rooftops on the other side of the square into glitter. The sun brings the stores—Backwoods Sport & Ski, Howe's Herbal Shoppe, and Tragic Ink—to life. Like a necromancer raising the dead. Darkness touched by light.

I have a lot of experience with darkness, with beasts, and with life. That's what happens when your psychic abilities are tied to evil.

Eloise calls what she does spiritually guiding people's lives.

I sentence them to damnation.

Spiritual writing, my aunt calls it. Communication from the dead translated through written words. It all sounds so harmless.

I was barely old enough to write when I scribed my first message. Wide-eyed and excited, I handed the note to a man in town, the words *u will die and deemuns will feest on ur sol* scrawled in crayon. As if this was a completely normal thing for a gap-toothed five-year-old girl to do. As if I was delivering a winning lottery ticket rather than a death sentence.

Turns out, people don't like knowing when they're going to die. They like even less knowing their souls are indulgent treats for demons.

The man cried. I didn't come out of my room for two days.

Worse yet, he was a mortal, and he *died*.

That night, the Court of the Sun and the Moon came for me, everyone solemn-faced and full of regret. A world of secrets was revealed—secrets about the town I lived in and the people I loved. Havenwood Falls, Colorado, is a sanctuary for people and creatures with supernatural abilities. It's also home to mortals. Oh, and ironically, demons, but not the kind of demons that like me. Not the soul-sucking terrible horrible creatures that I seem to channel.

The rules of our town are simple: protect the secret and don't kill the mortals.

At five years old, I was off to a bad start.

My aunt pats me on the cheek, breaking me out of my thoughts, her hand warm from the mug. "Hmm."

Nothing good ever comes from Eloise's hmms.

Snatching her mug, I gulp down the mugwort and bourbon. For the nerves, not the mental enhancement.

"It's a house," I say. Not just any house. *My* house. My first house. A place all my own, completely book- and writing-free. That's a lot more difficult than it sounds.

Words are everywhere. On television, clothes, signs, groceries, phones . . . the list goes on forever. I've trained myself to look at things without actually *looking* at them. If it's possible to avoid my "gift," then I do it.

The bell at the front of the store *dings.*

"You're not going to want the chamomile or candles," Eloise says from behind one of the displays. She doesn't have to see the customer to know why she's come. "It's oolong tea and a charged black tourmaline crystal for you. Trust me. You have all kinds of negative energy attached to you, and it is not good for your health."

At least her gift doesn't kill people.

I'm still stuck on Eloise's hmms.

The hmms chase me through the rest of the morning and through the streets of Havenwood Falls. It's too early for my meeting at the plaza when I leave my aunt's shop, so I am in no hurry when I hit Main Street on foot, my hands tucked deep within my coat pockets. I have a bad habit of facing my weaknesses while also avoiding them. This is why I find myself standing in front of Shelf Indulgence, a bookstore on Main Street, the smell of coffee wafting from Coffee Haven next door.

My eyes drift over the large showcase window so quickly that everything inside is merely a blur, before my gaze falls to my feet, puffs of air the only thing between me and the ground. Shelf Indulgence is my own personal hell. A place full of everything I wish I could touch and see. A place full of everything I wish I could *be*. The owner, a witch named Sedona Mathews, always decorates the showcase window with wildly creative displays. I'm both tempted and afraid to look at it. I am blind without being blind, my mind used to counting steps and knowing exactly where everything is, so that I can avoid anything new and potentially dangerous. My mind hates change, but my heart craves it.

"Harper?" a familiar female voice calls.

A pair of small brown boots settle next to mine on the sidewalk, and I let my gaze slide up them, over Thanksgiving-themed leggings and a long burgundy tunic to a pale face surrounded by silvery blond hair. Her skin positively glows. Concerned turquoise eyes stare at me. Willow Fairchild, the owner of Coffee Haven, and as of a few months ago, a new mother. Motherhood agrees with her.

She smiles. "It's been a few days since I saw you down this way. Do you have any new photographs for me? Your last set was popular with the customers."

I try to talk and can't, my words caught somewhere between the emotions building within me and the desire to walk inside Coffee Haven to see the new artwork Willow has displayed.

Silence stretches between us.

Reaching out, Willow squeezes my shoulder gently. "You let me know when you do, okay?" Profound understanding colors her eyes a deeper shade of turquoise, and I know she senses my unease and troubled thoughts. Willow, like many of the town's residents, is a supernatural, an empathetic fae with the power to sense emotions.

Throwing me a final smile, she enters Coffee Haven. A blast of warm air and the smell of blueberry scones hits me. I inhale, sucking in the scent and the warm feeling that comes with it.

Cars and pedestrians meander slowly around my spot on the sidewalk, and I turn away from the bookstore and coffee shop, my gaze settling on the town square across the street and a sparkling fountain in the distance. A work truck is parked near the curb, and a man leans against it, a cup of coffee cradled in his hands. Like with most of the locals, I've seen him before, but I don't know him. I'm not a social person, even though I think I could be if things were different.

This man is broad, a beard protecting his face from the cold, and he sips the coffee, watching me. When my eyes catch his, he pauses, dips his head, and lifts his cup. There are secrets lurking in his gaze, and even though it's unnerving to find him observing me, I don't feel threatened. I have a strange feeling he's studying me for the same reason I study him back. Secrets. There are secrets everywhere in this town.

Today, however, secrets are the least of my concerns. Today, I'm making Harper history. Giddy excitement fills me, the emotions overwhelming everything else, and I slip down the street. Away from the stranger. Away from Shelf Indulgence and my wishes. Away from Willow Fairchild and her empathetic understanding.

Away from everything I know and toward something new.

Purchase *Ink & Fire* at your favorite book retailer.